YORK NOTES

General Editors: Profes~~sor A.N. Jeffares~~ (*University of Stirling*) & Professor Suheil Bushrui (*American University of Beirut*)

Graham Greene

BRIGHTON ROCK

Notes by Michael Routh

MA (CALIFORNIA STATE UNIVERSITY, LONG BEACH)
PH D (WISCONSIN)

LONGMAN
YORK PRESS

YORK PRESS
Immeuble Esseily, Place Riad Solh, Beirut

LONGMAN GROUP UK LIMITED
Longman House, Burnt Mill, Harlow,
Essex CM20 2JE, England
Associated companies, branches and representatives
throughout the world

First published 1983
Fifth impression 1993

ISBN 0-582-02257-6

Printed in Hong Kong
WC/04

Contents

Part 1

Introduction

Biographical background

Like most writers, (Henry) Graham Greene (born 2 October 1904) was brought up in a middle-class family. His father was headmaster of a boarding-school in Berkhamsted, which young Greene himself attended. In a number of his non-fictional works Greene has described at some length the boredom, unhappiness, and even evil he suffered at Berkhamsted, and a good deal of his fiction, including *Brighton Rock* (1938), is marked by the theme of the lost innocence of childhood. As a schoolboy Greene toyed with a variety of methods of suicide; he eventually ran away to escape the miseries of school, as a result of which he underwent psychoanalysis. At Balliol College, Oxford, Greene read history, graduating in 1925 and publishing that year his first work, an undistinguished volume of verse. The following year Greene left the Anglican Church, in which he had been brought up, to become a Roman Catholic. He took up work as a journalist, and began writing his first novel, which appeared in 1929. Since that time, except for employment with the British Foreign Office during the Second World War, Greene has been a professional writer who, although known primarily as a novelist, has produced works in numerous genres. He has travelled the world accumulating material for his books.

Greene's fiction

Greene himself divides his work into two categories: (*a*) 'entertainments'; and (*b*) serious novels. The entertainments are, generally speaking, spy or detective stories utilising the essential ingredients of melodrama – rapidly paced narratives telling of capture and escape, flight and pursuit, violence and murder, all leading up to an action-packed climax. They concentrate on the criminal (the hunted) rather than on those hunting him, as is more usual in such stories. The serious novels, on the other hand, generally have as their focal point the Catholic theme. That is, instead of focusing primarily on the 'pot-boiler' or 'thriller' aspects of the tale, as he does in his entertainments, Greene in his serious novels deals above all else with such themes as sin and damnation, spiritual suffering, and the possibility of salvation.

In practice, however, Greene's fiction often combines these two modes. *Brighton Rock*, published first as an 'entertainment' in America but as a 'novel' in England, is the earliest example of this tendency to present the serious religious theme within the melodramatic framework of crime and detection. Such works appear at the start, and on the surface, to be conventional thrillers; but as each novel progresses, the fundamental seriousness of the narrative gradually emerges, so that what begins as melodrama (an adventure tale whose turbulent action is its own end) becomes elevated to tragedy (a story of great moral gravity whose action is only a means by which the author makes a significant statement about humanity). This is perhaps what Greene meant when he stated in an interview that 'melodrama is one of my working tools'. In any case, *Brighton Rock* exemplifies this gradual shift within a single work from melodrama to seriousness: the narrative's opening sentence announces the imminent murder of Hale, and it is not until about one-fifth of the way into the novel, when Pinkie and Rose reveal that they are both 'Romans', that the Catholic theme is introduced and the story begins to assume added significance.

The question at this point is why Greene chooses to yoke crime and detection with religion. One possible reason is that the detective story provides a fit metaphor with which to interpret spiritual crises: the surface tale of crime and punishment in the outer, physical world corresponds to the deeper working out of sin and damnation (or, through true repentance, salvation) in the inner, spiritual world. This might be a reason why Greene's fiction concentrates on the criminal, the one pursued: the framework of the thriller is an analogue for the inner pursuit by God of the soul of a spiritual outlaw who has joined in league with the devil. *Brighton Rock*, then, and such of Greene's other novels as combine their author's two modes, can be seen as allegories in that they are susceptible to a 'double reading' involving both the physical and the spiritual worlds. Greene has in fact written that murder, taken seriously, 'is a religious subject'.

Another possible related motive for Greene to link detection with religion is suggested by the allegorical tradition of 'wheat and chaff', according to which religious messages (the wheat, or fruit) are intentionally concealed by unimportant trappings (the chaff, or rind). In other words, a writer wanting to say something of great religious significance might do so disguisedly, by apparently saying something of only minimal worth. In this way, not only is the precious truth hidden from vulgar minds that might debase it, but also the difficulty inherent in searching out the real meaning concealed beneath the surface meaning helps to impress the truth, once discovered, firmly in the mind. Transposed to Greene's fiction, the suggestion is that he purposefully disguises religious 'wheat' by a superficial 'chaff' of adventure.

The Catholic theme

Although no critic ranks Greene with Joseph Conrad (1857–1924), D. H. Lawrence (1885–1930), Virginia Woolf (1882–1941), or E. M. Forster (1879–1970) among the leading twentieth-century English novelists, none the less Greene is perhaps the most artistically successful Catholic novelist England has produced. Some essential beliefs of Catholicism relevant to Greene's work are the following:

1. There is a God, whose ways are unknowable and whose judgements are inscrutable.
2. There is also a devil, or at least a negative force, who is responsible for evil in the world.
3. Man is tainted by Original Sin and is thus by nature weak.
4. There is an afterlife, consisting of either heaven (by way of purgatory) or hell.
5. Man's religious duty is to have faith in God.
6. The final judgement determining one's eternal position in heaven or hell will be made on the basis of one's faith or lack of faith.
7. The eighth, and the most deadly, sin is religious despair, the total loss of faith due to a mistaken conviction that God has abandoned one completely.
8. Suicide is the ultimate expression of despair and consequently the most damning action one can take.

In understanding Greene's use of religion in his fiction, it is helpful to know that when Greene was instructed in, and became converted to, Catholicism in the mid-1920s, the Roman Catholic Church was going through one of its most Jansenistic periods. Jansenism, a nonconformist movement within the Church, called after Cornelius Jansen (1585–1638), focuses on the gloomy, pessimistic, even morbid aspects of religion, emphasising what it considers to be man's innate perversity. At least in part, this accounts for the seeming predilection for suffering and the resultant dark atmosphere of *Brighton Rock* and other similar works by Greene.

A note on the text

Brighton Rock was first published in 1938 as a 'novel' in England, by Heinemann, London, and as an 'entertainment' in America, by Viking, New York. American reprints of *Brighton Rock* classify the work as a novel. Other useful editions are the following: volume seven of the Uniform Edition, Heinemann, London, 1950; and volume one of the Collected Edition, Heinemann and Bodley Head, London, 1970, which includes an Introduction by Greene. These Notes refer to the readily available Penguin edition of *Brighton Rock*, Harmondsworth, 1975.

Part 2

Summaries
of BRIGHTON ROCK

A general summary

Hale, a journalist working under the pseudonym 'Kolley Kibber' on a promotional stunt for his newspaper, is murdered by a race-track gang led by seventeen-year-old Pinkie Brown (the Boy) because the gang holds Hale responsible for the death of its former leader, Kite. Although the gang had strangled Hale with a piece of Brighton rock — hard stick-candy with the word BRIGHTON embedded through the length of it – the police record states that Hale died from heart failure brought on by the heat. However, Ida Arnold, who was with Hale just before he died, suspects foul play and sets out to bring Hale's murderer to justice. With increasing intensity, pressure is brought to bear upon Pinkie: Colleoni, a highly successful rival gang leader, tries to take over Pinkie's extortion racket; Ida finds more and more evidence of the Boy's guilt; and Pinkie unhappily realises that he must marry Rose Wilson, the sixteen-year-old waitress who saw one of his men trying to pass himself off as Kibber in an attempt to fabricate an alibi for the gang, to prevent her from being forced to testify against him. The gang begins to fall apart as, in a frenzied effort to ensure his own safety, Pinkie feels compelled to take more and more violent action, including the murder of a paranoid gang-member, who would, Pinkie feared, have led the police to him. But Ida catches up with Pinkie just as he is about to rid himself of Rose by talking her into committing suicide, and Pinkie leaps to his death. The novel ends with Rose, convinced of Pinkie's love for her, about to play his recorded message saying that he hates her.

Detailed summaries

Part One: 1

Aware that Pinkie Brown's mob, the Bookmakers' Protection, wants to kill him, 'Fred' Hale none the less moves about Brighton on Whitsun distributing 'Kolley Kibber' cards as part of a promotion for the *Daily Messenger* newspaper. Hale, small, timid, and nervous, is particularly vulnerable because the *Messenger* has printed a photograph of him and a time-table of his movements. Attracted by a woman's singing that he hears coming from a pub, Hale stops off for a drink. He at once takes a fancy to the singer, a buxom, well-preserved woman of about forty – Ida Arnold, a Londoner visiting Brighton for Whitsun. The seventeen-year-old Pinkie enters the bar, and Hale attempts to bribe the pale, physically immature boy with the reward money for the Kolley Kibber promotion. When Pinkie refuses and leaves, Hale realises that Pinkie's mob intends to kill him. He nervously continues his assignment of depositing his cards around Brighton, at the same time searching for a girl to pick up in the belief that he is safe as long as he is not alone. After several unsuccessful efforts, Hale finds Molly Pink, a working girl down from London for the holiday, who responds to his advances. Molly, however, wants a male companion for her friend, Delia, and, when Pinkie suddenly appears, thinks she has found one. Hale walks rapidly away. When he again hears Ida singing inside a pub, he enters the pub. She tells him that her former husband, Tom, wants her back, but that she is not interested in returning to him. Hale lies to Ida that his Christian name is Fred; he habitually hides his real name, Charles, from strangers. Hale then gives Ida a long-shot tip on a racehorse, Black Boy. Finally, he begs Ida to accompany him throughout the rest of the day, and she agrees. They hire a taxi, but are followed by Pinkie's Morris. After the taxi ride Ida leaves Hale briefly to wash; and, when she returns, he has disappeared.

NOTES AND GLOSSARY:

'This were . . . again': the novel's epigraph, or motto, from *The Witch of Edmonton* (1621), a tragi-comedy by Thomas Dekker (?1570–1632), John Ford (1586–?1639), and William Rowley (?1585–?1642); defining successful ruling as the ability to commit evil without paying retribution, the lines provide an ironic contrast for the story of the small-scale reign of terror for which Pinkie pays with his life

Brighton: on the coast of East Sussex, directly south of London, Brighton has been since the eighteenth century a popular and fashionable holiday resort; its race-track is one of its chief attractions

Whitsun: Pentecost, the seventh Sunday following Easter, which commemorates the descent of the Holy Spirit upon Christ's disciples (see the Bible, Acts 2)

Victoria: a main London railway station, from which trains leave for Brighton; named after Queen Victoria (reigned 1837–1901)

Victorian: characteristic of the reign of Queen Victoria (see above); as used here, the meaning of the adjective is unclear – perhaps it is meant to suggest middle-class respectability, which was prominent in the later nineteenth century and which Pinkie's mob will, shortly, violate brutally

sentry-go:
the duty of pacing up and down; the term is used loosely here

Kolley Kibber:
Colley Cibber (1671–1757), besides being a poet and playwright, was an actor popular for his comic interpretations of dandies and eccentrics; the allusion is perhaps meant to give comic overtones to Hale's character; moreover, Cibber's imperviousness to criticism stands in ironic opposition to Hale's vulnerability

shilling:
a former British unit of money worth one-twentieth of a pound

Southend:
Southend-on-Sea, Essex, a popular resort on the Thames estuary

guineas:
a guinea is worth one pound five pence

peepshows:
in a peepshow, a miniature picture is seen in perspective through a small hole in a box

'When I came up from Brighton by the train': one of the popular ballads Ida sings — simple, sentimental, romantic songs narrative in nature; the subject-matter of these ballads (a) helps to characterise Ida and (b) expresses conventional values that Pinkie finds repulsive

Guinness:
the name of a strong, dark beer brewed by the firm of Arthur Guinness in Dublin and elsewhere; Guinness is reputed to mellow the tone of a singer's voice

Lord Rothschild:
Lionel Walter Rothschild, Second Baron Rothschild (1868–1937), a distinguished member of Europe's best-known banking family; he was born and died in England. A baron is properly addressed as 'Lord'

Australian gold rush: the gold rush in Australia began in 1851

commissionaire:
a uniformed attendant; perhaps a member of the Corps of Commissionaires, pensioned soldiers who work as attendants at, for example, hotels and cinemas

pygmy:
here, dwarf

bob:
(slang) shilling (see above)

down:
soft hair; because it also means the first soft feathers of birds and the soft fuzz on some fruits, the word emphasises Pinkie's physical immaturity

buer's:
(slang) a buer is a whore

a fiver:	a five-pound note
Sheffield:	a manufacturing city in South Yorkshire, north of London
port:	a sweet, strong, usually dark red Portuguese wine
Bass:	an English beer
scamped:	performed in a superficial manner
cronies:	chums, friends
poisoned ambush:	some tribal natives of (usually) jungle areas surprise their enemies from hiding-places, attacking them with poison-tipped arrows or spears
pastiche:	something made up of material from a number of sources, or an imitation
ermine:	a type of weasel whose white winter fur is used for expensive women's coats
perm:	(*colloquial*) permanent wave: hair curled into waves lasting until the hair grows out
chestnut:	dark reddish-brown
macadam:	a road surface made up of broken stones
dowager:	the widow of a man of title; (*colloquial*) a well-to-do elderly woman
***en brosse*:**	(*French*) close-cropped
pillar-box:	a postbox in the form of a pillar
spotty:	having facial pimples
pastily:	with a pale face
splits:	a split is an ice-cream dish containing split fruit
ribald:	here, good-humouredly coarse
Ida:	the classical name of the highest mountain on the Grecian island of Crete, in a cave of which Zeus is said to have been reared; with its classical echo, the name (*a*) juxtaposes the secularism of Ida to the Catholicism of Pinkie and Rose; and (*b*) suggests Ida's role as a sort of Greek fury relentlessly avenging a deed of blood
tipsy:	(*slang*) slightly drunk
valley of the shadow:	a biblical echo; see Psalms 23:4: 'Yea, though I walk through the valley of the shadow of death, I will fear no evil: for thou [God] art with me; thy rod and thy staff they comfort me'
flutter:	(*colloquial*) small-scale betting
twenty to one:	the odds on Black Boy; one pound bet on him will, if he wins, return twenty pounds
a blow along the front:	a breath of fresh air on the promenade, which at a seaside resort faces the ocean
geezer:	(*slang*) fellow

Part One: 2

After the gang – Pinkie, Spicer, Cubitt and Dallow – has murdered Hale, Spicer places Kolley Kibber cards along Hale's route to disguise the time of the murder and Pinkie moves about Brighton establishing alibis. Meeting the other three for lunch at a tea-room, Pinkie learns that Spicer has made a potentially dangerous move by leaving a Kolley Kibber card at a restaurant, Snow's, at which he might have been noticed. Against the wishes of the mob, Pinkie goes to the restaurant to retrieve the card, but is too late. Rose, the girl who served Spicer, tells Pinkie that she took the card, but did not challenge the man who left it because he in no way resembled the photograph of Kibber printed in the *Messenger*. To protect himself Pinkie befriends the pale, thin, frightened Rose.

NOTES AND GLOSSARY:

the Boy:	for the first time 'Boy', in reference to Pinkie, is capitalised, as it is throughout the rest of the novel; since this episode marks the first appearance of Pinkie after the murder of Hale, the capitalisation is perhaps intended to suggest that Pinkie has made a perverse entry into the world of violent crime
slatey:	because the adjective derives from a type of grey slate, its use here emphasises Pinkie's inhumanity and rock-like insensitivity
quoits:	a game in which rings are thrown
repository:	storage place
Hail Mary . . . of our death:	the first and last words of one of the prayers from the Roman Catholic Mass
'I don't eat chocolates':	Greene is clearly trying to emphasise Pinkie's ascetic way of life, yet later, in Part Six: 2, Greene includes chocolate as part of Pinkie's normal diet
London time:	the time at the London borough of Greenwich is used as a basis for computing time in each of the world's twenty-four international time zones
hubbub:	confusing sounds
spew:	vomit
polony:	(*slang*) whore; from the name for Bologna sausage
a half:	ten shillings; a reference to the money Hale gave Ida at the end of Part One: 1
tarts:	(*slang*) women of loose sexual morals
vox humana:	(*Latin*) the voice of humanity
muddle:	blunder
dapper:	neat, smart

Part One: 3

Her holiday over, Ida has returned to London. At Henekey's bar she meets an old boy friend, Clarence, 'the ghost', who points out to her a newspaper story of Hale's death. The story reports that Hale died of natural causes; but Ida's instincts tell her something is amiss, and she is outraged that no questions were asked at Hale's inquest. After attending a highly commercialised funeral service for Hale, Ida decides to look more deeply into the matter of his death. An interview with Molly Pink, whose name and place of employment were given in the newspaper, convinces Ida that her suspicions about Hale's death are correct. In her flat she consults a planchette on the subject and, receiving further impetus from its revelations, vows to see that justice is done.

NOTES AND GLOSSARY:

the Strand:	a main street on the north bank of the Thames in central London; except where indicated, other place-names in this episode refer to locations in central London
Belisha beacons:	a Belisha beacon is a post topped by an amber light signifying a pedestrian crossing; named after Lord Hore-Belisha, who was appointed Minister of Transport in 1934
White Horse:	a brand of Scotch whisky
Ruby:	(*slang*) port wine (see earlier note on 'port', Part One: 1)
mug's:	(*slang*) fool's
Middlesbrough:	an industrial town in Cleveland, in northern England
Whit Monday:	the day after Whitsun; the context suggests that Hale was killed on Whit Monday, whereas the first paragraph of the novel gives Whitsun – a Sunday – as the day of his murder
Hove:	a resort town contiguous with Brighton
David Copperfield:	the reference is to the 1934 MGM film of Charles Dickens's (1818–70) novel of the same title (1849–50)
plus-fours:	baggy knickerbocker trousers
Bournemouth:	a seaside resort in Dorset, west of Brighton
hieroglyphics:	picture writing, a system of writing based on symbols rather than letters
Clapham:	a district of south-west London
the flickers:	(*slang*) the cinema
wireless set:	a radio

Midland Regional: a broadcasting station serving the Midland region of England

Calais: a seaport on the west coast of France; the woman could take a one-day holiday there because the crossing from England to Calais is the shortest

National Programme: the nation-wide broadcasting service, as against a regional one

cassock: a long clerical garment

New Art: more commonly known by its French name, '*art nouveau*'; a decorative style characterised by curving plant forms which was fashionable in the late nineteenth and early twentieth centuries

the old medieval beliefs in glassy seas and golden crowns: a simple picture of heaven with its saints; see the Bible, Revelations 4:4,6

Californian Poppy: an inexpensive brand of scent

ouija boards: a ouija board is a device used to obtain spiritual messages at séances (see below) by pointing to letters of the alphabet

Papists: the name given by English people to Roman Catholics, who swore allegiance to the Pope, rather than to the English king, after Henry VIII (reigned 1509–47) became head of the Anglican Church

ectoplasm: here, a semi-fluid which supposedly oozes from a spiritual medium

séances: gatherings for purposes of spiritual communication with the dead

the outsider . . . bobbing up: the long-shot race-horse you have bet money on passes the finishing line ahead of the other horses, and the colours associated with him are raised in victory

babble: speak foolishly

An eye for an eye: a biblical phrase, from Exodus 21:23–25: 'life for life, eye for eye, tooth for tooth, hand for hand, foot for foot, burning for burning, wound for wound, stripe for stripe'

Vengeance was Ida's: see the Bible, Romans 12:19: 'Vengeance is mine; I will repay, saith the Lord'.

carburettors: a carburettor is a part of a car engine

Stanley Gibbons: a specialist stamp collectors' shop

Edwardian moustache: a bushy style of moustache of the sort worn by Edward VII (reigned 1901–10)

dray: a low cart without sides used for hauling heavy loads; here, a horse-drawn cart

naffy suitings: smart clothes
raffish: dissipated
Epsom: a race course south-west of London
fizz: (*slang*) champagne
beggars: (*colloquial*) persons
two quid: 'quid' is slang for one pound sterling
***Woman and Beauty*:** a popular women's magazine
blarney: cajoling talk; those who kiss the blarney stone in County Cork, Ireland, are believed to acquire the gift of persuasive, if deceitful or even nonsensical, speech
dunning: pestering; a 'dun' is a debt-collector who exerts great pressure in collecting money
the Board: a planchette, which when touched supposedly writes spiritual messages automatically
Eastbourne: a seaside resort in East Sussex, to the east of Brighton
Hastings: another East Sussex seaside resort, east of Eastbourne
Aberystwyth: a seaside resort on the central coast of Wales
An Edgar Wallace: a novel by Edgar Wallace (1875–1932), author of numerous popular 'thrillers'; an essay by Greene on Wallace as a writer of popular novels appears in Greene's *Collected Essays*
a Netta Syrett: a work by a popular novelist of the time
***The Good Companions*:** a picaresque novel (1929) that made its author, J. B. Priestley (1894–1984), successful with the popular audience
***Sorrell and Son*:** the best-known work of Warwick Deeping (1877–1950), a writer of popular sentimental novels; Ida's library, revealing her sentimental taste, reinforces her characterisation
pit-pony eyes: used for haulage in mines, pit ponies were kept underground and therefore often went blind
netty: net-like, made of net
prow: front section
plumes: large ornamental feathers
foolscap: a long sheet of writing-paper
Warwick Deeping: see note to '*Sorrell and Son*', above

Part Two: 1

A week after the murder of Hale, Pinkie believes that Spicer's paranoia threatens the mob. The Boy discloses to Spicer that, instead of a knife or a pistol, he carries a bottle of vitriol in his pocket. When Rose comes to meet Pinkie for a date, as both a threat and a warning he demonstrates to her the destructive power of vitriol. The two go to Sherry's, a dance hall. There Pinkie reveals an obsessive susceptibility to music; learns that, like himself, Rose is a Roman Catholic; confides that he was once a choirboy; and expresses a firm belief in hell, but not in heaven.

Returning to his room at Frank's, Pinkie learns from his mob that two of the bookmakers who pay his gang for 'protection' have refused to settle their subscriptions. Moreover, the Boy is infuriated to find that, in his absence, the members of the mob have been amusing themselves at his expense over a joke of Spicer's that Pinkie will marry Rose. Pinkie and Dallow call on one of the bookmakers, Bill Brewer, who tells them that he and the other bookmaker, Jim Tate, are now paying protection money to Colleoni, a high-class mobster who is attempting to take over Pinkie's territory. Pinkie slashes Brewer's face with a razor and collects the subscription money. Back in his room, Pinkie learns from the increasingly nervous Spicer that a woman (Ida, of course) has been asking Rose questions at Snow's Restaurant. Pinkie orders Spicer to take a holiday.

NOTES AND GLOSSARY:

catgut:	the dried and twisted intestines of (usually) sheep used to make violin strings
milky:	(*slang*) soft, effeminate
vitriol:	concentrated sulphuric acid; since in popular belief the fires of hell were thought to be of sulphur, Pinkie's demonic nature is emphasised by his carrying vitriol
blower:	(*slang*) telephone
Three sixes:	666, the devil's number (see the Bible, Revelations 13:18), again emphasising Pinkie's hellishness
rumba:	a popular ballroom dance of the 1930s imitating an Afro-Cuban folk dance
unfledged:	(*figurative*) immature, inexperienced; from 'fledged', referring to a bird old enough to fly
Everest:	the name of a commercial brand of ice-cream
two-backed beasts:	a man and a woman dancing; but the phrase echoes the villain Iago's words describing sexual intercourse in Shakespeare's tragedy *Othello*: 'I am one, sir, that comes to tell you, your daughter and the Moor are

now making the beast with two backs' (I.1.116–17); that a Shakespearean reference would enter Pinkie's consciousness is, of course, highly improbable

cabaret: floor-show entertainment

crooner: a singer of popular, sentimental songs sung in a low, soft voice, using a microphone

starling: a type of small bird that sings throughout the year

the anthem ... to stone: the national anthem is played on the second Sunday in November, formerly known as Armistice Day, which originally commemorated those who died in the First World War (concluded by truce, or armistice, on 11 November 1918); on this day the British monarch (George VI at the time of the action of *Brighton Rock*) lays a flower wreath on the Cenotaph (war memorial in Whitehall) while spectators respectfully remove their hats and the troops stand at attention; because today it commemorates those who died in the Second World War, as well as those who died in the First, Armistice Day is now known as Remembrance Sunday

Gracie Fields: an immensely popular comedienne (1898–1980) known for the irreverent humour of her songs

Chinese lanterns: collapsible lampshades made from coloured paper

green: (*figurative*) inexperienced; from the colour of unripe fruit

council school: locally run free school

'Oh,' she said, ... 'go on': Pinkie's sadism here is complemented by Rose's masochism

Woolworth: a chain of inexpensive department stores

string of beads: a rosary, used to count the prayers to the Virgin Mary in Roman Catholic ritual

Roman: shortened form of Roman Catholic

'Agnus dei ... dona nobis pacem': from a hymn from the Latin Mass: 'Lamb of God, who takes away the sins of the world, grant us peace'

credo in unum Dominum: also from a hymn from the Latin Mass: 'I believe in one Master'; see Part Six: 2

unmatted flight: a staircase without floor-covering

subscriptions: fees for 'protection', paid to Pinkie's mob

carve: (*slang*) to cut with a razor

jerry: a chamber pot, a bowl used as a urinal

sub.: an abbreviated form of 'subscription' (see note above)

ague:	a malarial fever; used figuratively here. Throughout the novel Pinkie is associated with sickness and disease
A clock struck midnight:	as a clock strikes eleven p.m. while Pinkie is with Spicer, before Rose comes, the time here could hardly be only one hour later
clapper:	normally, colloquial for 'tongue'; but here apparently used to mean 'mouth'
shell case:	the outer case, or cartridge, of an explosive
ferns:	a fern is a type of plant with feather-like leaves
welsher:	(*slang*) someone who does not pay off a bet he has lost
bobble fringe:	an ornamental border with woolly balls
sideboard:	a piece of furniture that serves as both side-table and cupboard
bogies:	(*slang*) police
Whitehawk Bottom:	the foot of the Downs close to Brighton race course
the monoliths of Stonehenge:	a prehistoric monument of large stones arranged by the Celts in concentric circles on Salisbury Plain, Wiltshire
Boulogne:	Boulogne-sur-mer, a French seaport across the English Channel from Brighton

---

Part Two: 2

Pinkie goes to the fashionable Cosmopolitan Hotel at the request of Colleoni, who has called the meeting to warn Pinkie against harming bookmakers such as Brewer, who now pay Colleoni's mob for protection. Colleoni also tries to persuade the Boy to turn the race-track protection business completely over to him, but Pinkie refuses. On his way out, Pinkie is taken into custody by the police. The police inspector also warns him to abandon his racket to Colleoni. These two confrontations stimulate Pinkie's murderous impulses.

NOTES AND GLOSSARY:

the falling ... time exposure:	in time-lapse photography, the camera's shutter admits light over a period of time (and not for only an instant, as in normal photography), so that, for example, the blossoming of a flower can be filmed; the photographic process is ended by the pressing of a bulb, which closes the camera's shutter
mauve:	pale shade of purple
cachou:	lozenge for sweetening the breath
tinted creatures:	women with dyed hair

bitch: (*vulgar*) woman; from the name for a female dog – hence the verb 'sniffed'

settee: a long seat with a back

Louis Seize: an ornate style of neoclassical art – here, of furniture and architecture – fashionable during the reign of Louis XVI (reigned 1774–93)

glacé: made of thin glossy leather

Pompadour Boudoir: a boudoir is a small, private room; Madame de Pompadour (1721–64) was a mistress of Louis XV, king of France (reigned 1715–74)

tiara: a woman's ornamental jewelled headband; 'untimely' perhaps because it is too formal a dress item to suit the situation here

chinoserie: chinoiserie is a decorative seventeenth- and eighteenth-century European furniture style imitative of Chinese design

hallmark: the official stamp of the Goldsmiths' Hall certifying the genuineness of an article made of gold

wide seaward windows: Colleoni's room is on the expensive side of the hotel, overlooking the sea; compare with the view Pinkie has from the window of his squalid room

Napoleonic: a nineteenth-century decorative style based on motifs popular during the reign of Napoleon Bonaparte, emperor of France (1804–15)

musk: a strong, expensive perfume obtained from the male musk-deer or from a musk-plant

lapped: enfolded

Greenwich: see the earlier note to 'London time', Part One: 2

grubby: dirty, grimy; a grub is the larva of an insect

half-crown enclosures: an enclosed place at a race-track for customers paying a half-crown, or two shillings and sixpence

Napoleon the Third: emperor of France (reigned 1852–70)

Eugenie: wife of Napoleon III (1826–1920) and empress of France (1853–70); Colleoni's ability to identify Eugenie only as 'one of those foreign polonies' suggests the ignorance and coarseness beneath his glittering surface

seraglio: (*Italian*) here used as slang for 'brothel'; otherwise, 'harem'

the Big Four: the four principal detectives at Scotland Yard police headquarters in London in the 1930s

wide: (*slang*) shrewd

the tote: the totalisation board, on which bets made at a race-track are registered

Players:	a brand of English cigarette produced by the firm of John Player
aertex:	loosely woven cotton fabric
He trailed ... in his infancy:	a reference to the 'Ode: Intimations of Immortality', by William Wordsworth (1770–1850): 'Not in entire forgetfulness,/And not in utter nakedness,/But trailing clouds of glory do we come/From God, who is our home:/Heaven lies about us in our infancy!'; Wordsworth's innocent child is blessed with a divine intuition of his heavenly pre-existence – but the satanic Pinkie is cursed with a demonic background

---

Part Three: 1

Ida has taken a cheap room in Brighton in order to look into Hale's death. Knowing that she will need more money than she has got to carry out her investigation, she places a large bet on a race horse, Black Boy, the tip Hale had given her. From a barman, Ida learns that Pinkie inherited his mob from its former leader, Kite, who was murdered by Colleoni's men (presumably for trying to move in on Colleoni's automatic-machines racket; Hale was murdered for betraying Kite to Colleoni [Part Two: 2]). While waiting in Snow's to meet a friend, Phil Corkery, who is also staying in Brighton, Ida questions Rose and has her suspicions strengthened.

Ida goes to the police. But when the inspector refuses to re-open Hale's case, she becomes even more determined that justice should be done.

NOTES AND GLOSSARY:

ewer:	a large water-jug
dithering:	trembling with nervous anticipation
barometer:	a device that, by measuring atmospheric pressure, is used to forecast the weather
sandshoes:	shoes made of canvas or rubber, used for walking on a beach
querulous:	whining
sinews of war:	money used for waging war; used figuratively here, for Ida consistently perceives her pursuit of Pinkie in military terms
Kemp Town:	an area of Brighton
Gold Flake:	a brand of cigarette
Douro port:	a wine produced in the province of Douro in northern Portugal

'Who *was* Kite? . . . St Pancras':the murder of Kite is described by Raven, who killed him, in Greene's *A Gun for Sale* (1936; American title: *This Gun for Hire*), Chapter V: 1; 'Battling Kite' was murdered because he tried to kill the leader of Raven's gang (but Colleoni is not mentioned); further, Raven says that the death of Kite was not a mistake (as the barman tells Ida he thinks it was)

St Pancras: a railway and underground station in central London

Rottingdean: a seaside resort slightly east of Brighton

larrup: (*colloquial*) spank, whip, thrash

dregs: sediment

shepherd's pie: a savoury pie, made of mashed potatoes over minced meat

stout: a strong dark beer

'Waste not, want not': a proverb, dating from the eighteenth century

a blazer with a badge: a blazer is a sports jacket, of the colours of some club or school, whose badge is on the jacket's left breast pocket

wake: pattern of water caused by a moving ship; in Part Four: 2 Ida is compared with a 'warship' as Greene develops *Brighton Rock's* battle imagery

brassy: (*slang*) impudent, presumptuous, cheeky

Camaraderie: (*French*) loyal and trusting fellowship

Appendix scar: Hale had had his appendix – a small, closed tube in the crotch area on the right side – surgically removed

supernumerary nipples: Hale had at least one additional nipple

Bank Holiday: a public holiday, on which all banks are closed by statute

varicose: abnormally enlarged

a bit lit: (*slang*) slightly drunk

'I've told you, Mrs Arnold, the case is closed': there is a suggestion of cover-up in the police's refusal to consider the possibility that Hale was murdered; not only do the police work with Colleoni in trying to persuade Pinkie to abandon the race-track racket (Part Two: 2), but the police are also said later in the novel to trust Colleoni greatly (Part Six: 1)

penny peep: (*colloquial*) a peepshow (see earlier note to Part One: 1) costing one penny for admittance

French polish: shellac

huckster: a pedlar of small goods

cannon fodder: (*figurative*) soldiers who are regarded solely as material to be used in a war; 'fodder' is cattle food

---

Part Three: 2

His paranoia increasing, Spicer moves anxiously from one locale associated with Hale's murder to another. He runs into Crab, a former member of Bookmakers' Protection now working for Colleoni. Crab informs Spicer that Pinkie is at the moment in the custody of the police. (Thus, this episode occurs simultaneously with the second half of Part Two: 2.) Back at Frank's, Spicer answers a frantic telephone call from Rose, who tells him that a woman (again, Ida) has been questioning her about the crime. Again walking about Brighton, Spicer unknowingly has his photograph taken under the pier and once again returns to the scene of the murder.

NOTES AND GLOSSARY:

nicotined finger-ends: nicotine is a poison in tobacco causing yellowish stains on the fingers of heavy cigarette smokers; see the description of Charlie Moyne's moustache, Part One: 3

shingle: seashore pebbles

lamp: (*slang*) know, recognise

mug: (*slang*) face

nark: (*slang*) a police spy or informer

grassed: (*slang*) informed against

squeal: (*slang*) inform against

Nottingham: an industrial city in Nottinghamshire, north of London

gaff: (*slang*) a cheap theatre or music-hall

the vulcanite: the telephone, which is made from vulcanite, rubber treated with sulphur to produce a hard, black material

a little moisture . . . ducts: an inflated way of saying that Spicer is beginning to weep; the language here is adjusted to Spicer's sentimental state of mind
ducts: tubes carrying bodily secretions – here, tear ducts

scuffling: probably should read 'scuffing': dragging one's feet

nave: the main part of a church, running from the entrance to the chancel; it is separated from the aisles by pillars, which support the roof, as the two rows of iron piles carry the pier; the image recurs in Part Five: 1

the drop: the falling, or dropping, of a criminal when hanged

Part Three: 3

At Snow's Pinkie feels insulted that he is not served as he waits for Rose. He takes Rose to Peacehaven, outside Brighton, where she tells him that Ida has been questioning her. Remembering that it is Saturday, Pinkie, who has never kissed a girl, recalls his parents' weekly, and to him frightening, sexual acts, which he regularly witnessed on Saturdays. The Boy realises that he must appease Rose in order to prevent her from going to the police. Having returned to Brighton because Pinkie is bored in the country, the two see Spicer's picture at a photographer's kiosk. Pinkie tries to claim the photo, but is turned away.

NOTES AND GLOSSARY:

The poison twisted in the Boy's veins: the suggestion here, and elsewhere in the novel, is that Pinkie is possessed of Original Sin (the Christian belief that, due to Adam's fall in the Garden of Eden, mankind is cursed from birth with innate evil)

Peacehaven: a suburban development east of Brighton

glands: organs that secrete vital bodily fluids and discharge them into or outside of the body; again, Pinkie's intrinsic malice is emphasised, for the products of his glands are 'poison'

mousy: dull brown or dark grey tinged with yellow – a characteristically unattractive colour for Rose's hair

Saxon emblems: early carvings in the chalk soil of the Downs, representing men or animals

the downs: the Downs are the chalk hills of southern England

Mazawattee: a brand-name of tea

giddy: dizzy, suffering from vertigo

the draught might never be offered: (*figurative*) the need to kill Rose might not arise

draught: an amount drunk at one time; although it seems to come from Pinkie's consciousness, the statement is too poetic for him, and a non-drinker such as Pinkie would not be likely to think in terms of a 'draught'

ruts: grooves made by erosion

'The pub's closed': a curious reason for Pinkie, who does not drink, to dislike the country

'Between the stirrup... something found': 'My friend, judge not me,/Thou seest I judge not thee./Betwixt the stirrup and the ground/Mercy I asked, mercy I found.' William Camden (1551–1623), *Remains,*

	'Epitaph for a Man Killed by Falling from His Horse'; significantly, Pinkie has forgotten the key word 'mercy', which, again significantly, Rose supplies
paddock:	here, a toad or frog
nape:	back of the neck
kiosk:	a small, open stall for selling goods
hypo:	hyposulphate, or sodium thiosulphate, a salt used in fixing, or making fast, photographic prints and negatives; it is doubtful that Pinkie would have been able to identify the odour
a by-your-leave:	permission
King Edward VIII:	Prince Edward, Duke of Windsor (1894–1972), became Prince of Wales in 1911 and was King Edward VIII from January to December 1936
peep machines:	devices used for peep-shows (see earlier note on 'peepshows', Part One: 1)
Vesta Tilley:	stage name of Matilda Alice Powles (1864–1952), a comedienne famous for her male impersonations
Henry Irving:	English Shakespearean actor (1838–1905)
Lily Langtry:	Lillie Langtry (1853–1929), an actress renowned for her beauty, who numbered among her admirers King Edward VII
Mrs Pankhurst:	the married name of Emmeline Goulden (1857–1928), for forty years an outspoken suffragette often jailed for her militancy
hobble skirts:	long, narrow women's skirts, popular before the First World War

Part Three: 4

Pinkie's fear that Spicer's obsessive paranoia will cause the latter to act in a rash manner dangerous to the whole gang comes to a head during a confrontation between the two at Frank's. Pinkie insists that Spicer leave town, but that he first accompany Pinkie to the races the following day. At this point, the Boy realises that Spicer must die. Pinkie phones Colleoni to arrange for Spicer to be murdered at the race-track. Colleoni's vague laughter at the close of the conversation and his abrupt manner of hanging up, however, leave Pinkie uneasy.

NOTES AND GLOSSARY:

leather-jacket:	crane fly ('leather-jacket' is actually the name for the larva of this insect)
deal:	fir or pine wood
smut:	a mark or smudge made by a piece of soot

a glassy sea, a golden crown, old Spicer: see the note on 'old medieval beliefs . . . golden crowns', Part 1: 3, above, which this echoes

free house: a public house licensed to sell several brands of beer (as opposed to a 'tied house', which is owned or run by a brewery to sell its beer only)

calcined: dried, hardened

thés dansants: (*French*) tea with dancing

a glass chink and ice move in a shaker: Colleoni is having a drink as he talks to Pinkie

chink: the sound drinking glasses make when struck together

shaker: container in which drinks are mixed

novis: should read 'nobis'

Part Four: 1

On the day of the races, Pinkie takes Spicer to the track to betray him to Colleoni's men. Black Boy, the tip Hale had given Ida, wins, paying off handsomely. Pinkie escorts Spicer to the scene of the arranged attack, only to find that Colleoni has crossed him: Colleoni's mob attacks Pinkie as well as Spicer. Humiliated and physically wounded, Pinkie escapes, eventually making his way to Snow's. In the restaurant's cellar, as Rose attends to his wounds, he continues to act in his forced conciliatory manner toward her. He realises that she, ironically, has power over him and that therefore he hates her. He decides that, because a wife cannot be forced to testify in a court of law against her husband, he must marry Rose for his own protection. Feeling that he is losing control of his own affairs, Pinkie returns to his room to have his lawyer, Prewitt, summoned about arranging a marriage with Rose.

Prewitt explains the difficulties concerning the marriage, and the possible solutions to them. Then Pinkie learns that Spicer, whom he had thought Colleoni's men had murdered at the race-track, is in his own room at Frank's.

NOTES AND GLOSSARY:

touch wood: a game in which a player who touches wood cannot be pursued

Indian file: several persons moving in a single line, one behind the other, in the manner of American Indians

tiger skin: worn over his uniform by the drum-major of a military band

pit ponies: see earlier note for 'pit-pony eyes', Part One: 3

Packard: an expensive American automobile, no longer made but fashionable at the time of the story

members' enclosure: a fenced-off section of a race-course reserved for special persons

Underground staircase: an escalator, or moving staircase, from an underground railway

fiver: (*colloquial*) a five-pound note

rakish: smart- and fast-looking, built for speed

totsies: (*colloquial*) girls

by-lanes: side-roads

Great North Road: at the time of the novel's action, the main road north out of London

ordure: dung

a cruel child . . . behind him: in his Prologue to *The Lawless Roads* (1936) Greene, discussing the tribulations of his boyhood experiences at boarding school, mentions 'Collifax who practised torments with dividers'
dividers: a measuring compass having sharp points

bitter: a light beer

the second coming: the Second Advent, the return of Jesus Christ to earth to judge mankind at the end of the world

tied house: see earlier note for 'free house', Part Three: 4

plantains: a common wild plant

Clapton: an area of east London

Memento Mori: (*Latin*) 'remember you must die'; a grimly ironic name for the horse the ill-fated Spicer believes will bring him luck

a pony: (*slang*) twenty-five pounds; but Spicer is mistaken: Ida in fact bet twenty pounds on Black Boy (Part Three: 1)

canter: an easy gallop

tic-tacked: signalled a change in the betting odds to another bookmaker by a systematic movement of the arms

masonic passes: secret signals; a reference to Freemasonry, a worldwide secret society for men

Whit Monday: like the reference to the day of Hale's murder in Part One: 3, this too contradicts what was said in the novel's first paragraph

the censor swung . . . the Host: in Pinkie's mind the high point of the Mass, the elevation of the Host, becomes confused with the dramatic finish of the race

touch wood . . . under ladders: popular superstitions relating to good and bad luck

A tenner: (*colloquial*) a ten-pound note

tout: a racing touter, one who for a price provides tips on horses

Shoreham:	Shoreham-by-Sea, a town west of Brighton
potting shed:	a small, usually wooden building in which sensitive plants are raised in pots until they are ready to be transplanted outside
pram:	(*colloquial abbreviation*) perambulator, a light, hand-pushed baby carriage
trowels:	a trowel is a small gardening tool used for digging
jackdaw:	a thievish type of bird
Doncaster . . . Northampton:	Lichfield is a market town; Clacton-on-Sea is a popular resort; the other places are larger provincial towns
tits:	(*vulgar*) female breasts
the statue:	the statue of a saint in a Catholic church
the bright lights . . . pink glasses:	candles lit in glass containers before the altar
Lancia:	an expensive Italian-made motor-car
waistcoat:	a sleeveless, buttoned men's garment worn over a shirt and under a jacket
tycoon:	(*colloquial*) a wealthy and powerful businessman
the alignments at Waterloo:	the military strategy involved in the battle of Waterloo (1815), in which British troops under the Duke of Wellington defeated Napoleon; although it is difficult to imagine Pinkie thinking in such historical terms, his doing so here reinforces the novel's battle imagery
the extras:	special issues of the racing newspapers
dolled up:	(*colloquial*) smartly dressed
paint:	coloured facial cosmetic
henna:	a reddish hair dye, so-called from the Asiatic shrub from which it is obtained
skirt:	(*slang*) woman
smutty:	(*figurative*) obscene; smut is a mark made by soot
Catherine wheel:	a firework that rotates while burning
bed-sitting room:	a single room that serves as both bedroom and sitting-room
carious:	decayed
phallic:	penis-like
dockside manner:	a borrowing from 'bedside manner', the way in which a doctor handles a bed-ridden patient; the dock is the courtroom enclosure for criminals
flint:	a type of hard stone; perhaps the reference here is to a tool or a weapon made by prehistoric man
calling a hand:	in card-playing, naming one of the four suits (spades, hearts, clubs, diamonds)

Canterbury Cathedral: Canterbury in the county of Kent is the ecclesiastical centre of the Anglican Church; Canterbury's archbishop, or head bishop, is 'primate of all England'

misdemeanour: an indictable offence against the law; at the time of *Brighton Rock* a misdemeanour was a less serious offence than a felony, a graver crime usually involving violence

civil marriage: a marriage solemnised by civil contract, as opposed to by religious ritual

fifteen days' residence: the minimum length of residence in a district or a city required for a licence to marry in that district

one day's notice: notice of a forthcoming marriage must be posted twenty-four hours before the ceremony

guardian: here, an adult having legal custody of an orphaned minor

tartar-coated: crusted over with calcium phosphate deposits

silver wedding: the twenty-fifth wedding anniversary

spliced: (*colloquial*) married

eiderdown: a quilt stuffed with the feathers of the eider duck

cockney: a pejorative term suggesting Rose's lower-class origins; the word may derive from 'cock's egg', a small, misshapen egg, and so here may be meant to emphasise these characteristics of Rose's face

---

Part Four: 2

Meanwhile, Ida continues her relentless pursuit of Rose because, Ida claims, she wants to save the girl from Pinkie. Cornering Rose in her room at Snow's, Ida tells her that Pinkie in reality does not love her; but Rose refuses to listen.

NOTES AND GLOSSARY:

a war to end wars: in the Bible, 'the battle of that great day [Judgement Day] of God Almighty' is to be fought at Armageddon (Revelation 16:14–16)

signal flags: flags used in the British Navy to signal messages

a public: (*colloquial*) public house; the implication is that Ida was formerly a prostitute

'I don't want the Innocent to suffer': the Holy Innocents were the children killed by Herod in his attempt to slay the Christ child (see the Bible, Matthew 2:16–18)

a Puritan: used colloquially here to mean one who rigidly opposes pleasures of the flesh; historically, Puritan opposition to Catholicism helped bring about the

Reformation in the sixteenth century, but Ida's opposition to the Catholics Rose and Pinkie is wholly secular

girdle of Venus: a line on the palm of the hand said by palmists to indicate a highly strung, nervous character with a tendency toward hysteria and despondency; yet Ida seems to think the girdle of Venus suggests a sexually active personality, presumably because Venus is the Roman goddess of sensual love and fertility

---

Part Four: 3

At the same time that Ida is confronting Rose, at Frank's Pinkie has pushed Spicer down several flights of stairs to his death. After forcing Prewitt to lie about the circumstances of Spicer's death, Pinkie leaves for Snow's to inform Rose of their coming marriage. At the restaurant he finds Ida badgering Rose. Rose continues to defy Ida, who soon leaves. Pinkie announces to Rose that they are to be married.

NOTES AND GLOSSARY:

Prometheus: a mythological figure who, because he gave mankind fire, was condemned by Zeus to be chained to a rock, there to have his liver eaten out daily by a vulture and restored each night

inner circle: a circular line on the London Underground system

Notting Hill: an area of London west of the centre

foxed: discoloured with fox-marks, yellowish-brown stains caused by dampness

Van Tromp's victory: referring to the Dutch admiral Maarten van Tromp (1597–1653); the engraving is either of his defeat of the Spanish in English waters in 1639, or of his defeat of English forces in the First Dutch War in 1652

his hard puritanical mouth: Pinkie's revulsion to sexual contact contrasts with Ida's non-Puritanical enjoyment of it; see earlier note for 'a Puritan', Part Four: 2

Coty powder: a brand of face powder

Kissproof Lipstick: brand of indelible lipstick

alms: money given to charity

Part Five: 1

Pinkie is increasingly disturbed by the apparently unending chain of events set into motion by his murder of Hale, and is by now himself paranoid. He reveals to Dallow – the only member of his gang he still trusts – the motive for Hale's murder. Hale had betrayed to Colleoni the gang's former leader, Kite, who was also a father-figure to Pinkie. Pinkie accompanies Dallow and Cubitt to a road-house out in the country, where Pinkie has his first drink. Pinkie, a virgin, seduces Sylvie, Spicer's girl, only to find himself humiliatingly impotent at the crucial moment.

NOTES AND GLOSSARY:

barques: a barque is a small sailing vessel

cuttle fish: a tentacled mollusc which, when pursued, ejects a black fluid

half-vulture and half-dove: a paradox: a vulture is a bird of prey, whereas a dove is traditionally a symbol of peace and innocence

road-house: an inn located on a main road in the country

arterial road: a main road with branches; the adjective 'arterial' derives from 'artery', a tube by which blood is carried to all parts of the body

a hoarding: a wooden fence either surrounding a construction site, or used for displaying advertisements

dicky: a folding seat at the back of a motor-car

Tudor barn: a barn in the architectural style popular during the reign of the Tudor monarchs (1485–1603)

paddock: here, a small enclosed field where horses are kept or exercised

clapping: (*slang*) talking

Sidecar: a cocktail made from orange liqueur, lemon juice and brandy

lamp: (*slang*) look at, see

clacked: made a rattling sound

gin slings: gin sling is an iced drink made of sweetened and flavoured gin

parquet: expensive, geometrically patterned hardwood flooring

retched: vomited, involuntarily made the sound and motion of vomiting

bathing-slip: bathing suit

The Boy stood . . . shining tiles: perhaps a parody of the Narcissus legend of classical mythology: Narcissus loved nobody until he saw his own beautiful image reflected back at him from a forest pool; but Pinkie, who is also aloof, sees only his own unattractive form reflected in the swimming pool, an image broken by the strokes of the swimmers (see note below for 'Narcissus', Part Six: 1)

Part Five: 2

On the way back from the road-house, Pinkie assures Dallow and Cubitt that he is not going to marry Rose. Arriving at Frank's, Pinkie finds Rose there; she has been fired from Snow's for being rude to a customer, the persistent, unrelenting Ida. Pinkie feels threatened by Rose's knowledge of Spicer's role in the murder of Hale, especially because her naivety makes her unpredictable – as when she asks Pinkie whether she ought to tell the police that it was Spicer who left the Kolley Kibber card at Snow's. Now Pinkie realises that he has no choice but to marry Rose.

NOTES AND GLOSSARY:

flask:	a pocket-bottle
a squint:	a sidelong, stealthy glance
submarine light:	the dim street lights are compared here to underwater lighting
Worthington:	a brand of English beer
spry:	vigorous, lively
Q ship:	a warship disguised as a non-combat vessel during the First World War; also called a 'mystery-ship'
magistrate's:	a magistrate is a civil officer who administers the law

Part Five: 3

On his way to the house of Rose's parents, where he has sent Rose, Pinkie passes through the impoverished neighbourhood he grew up in, Paradise Piece, which represents to him all that he wishes to rise above. Rose is from a similar neighbourhood, Nelson Place, so that her existence is a constant and bitter reminder to the Boy of his lower-class origins. At Rose's house, Pinkie eventually succeeds in buying, for fifteen guineas, Rose's parents' consent to her marriage to him.

NOTES AND GLOSSARY:

verdigrised:	(of copper) turned a greenish colour
Hostel:	here used in the archaic sense of 'inn'
treble:	a high-pitched child's voice
truck:	dealings
guineas:	a guinea is worth one pound and five pence

Part Five: 4

Meanwhile, Ida has taken a room at the high-class Cosmopolitan Hotel with her winnings on Black Boy. She re-affirms to the timid Phil her desire to hunt down Hale's murderer, then prepares to let Phil seduce her.

NOTES AND GLOSSARY:

éclair:	a rich iced pastry, filled with custard or cream
boskages:	a boskage is a wooded area of thick foliage
padding:	walking softly
Distinguay:	*distingué* (*French*): having a distinguished air
hothouse:	an artificially heated glass building, used for growing plants in cold climates; fruit grown in such buildings is expensive
Bacchic:	orgiastic; Bacchus, the Greek and Roman god of wine, was identified with Dionysus, a Greek god of fertility and of wine
bawdy:	humorously vulgar

Part Five: 5

Pinkie returns to his room to find the mob gathered for a pre-marriage bachelor party. Pinkie defends Rose before the others. Cubitt presents him with two obscene wedding presents, which revolt the Boy. When Pinkie threatens him, Cubitt quits the mob and leaves Frank's. Prewitt is telephoned to arrange the marriage, which will take place in two days' time.

NOTES AND GLOSSARY:

Her Titian hair was brown at the roots: Judy's hair has been dyed red, but is starting to grow out, revealing its actual colour; the description helps to characterise Judy as vulgar; *Titian* (?1490–1576): great Venetian Renaissance painter whose pictures often have figures with bright golden red-brown hair (known today as 'Titian red', the colour Judy has dyed her hair)

mascara'd:	artificially coloured
moued:	(*French*) pouted
kip:	(*slang*) cheap lodging-house
laying:	(*slang*) having sexual intercourse with
rough houses:	(*slang*) fights

that one dirty scramble: the sex act, which to the puritanical Pinkie is unclean

Grand Canyon:	a huge gorge, two hundred and seventeen miles long and four to fifteen miles wide, in the south-western American state of Arizona; the angular shapes and reddish colourings of its rocks are famous
Taj Mahal:	a magnificent mid-seventeenth-century mausoleum in India, built in memory of Arumand Banu Begam, who was called Mumtaz Mahal ('Chosen One of the Palace'), wife of the emperor Shah Jahan

| haemophilia: | 'bleeder's disease', an hereditary affliction in which, because the victim's blood does not clot, a very small cut causes severe bleeding |

Part Five: 6

Disappointed sexually by Phil, Ida returns with enthusiasm to contemplating her 'mission'. She decides that to forward her investigation she must talk to one of Pinkie's men.

NOTES AND GLOSSARY:

Bohemian:	easy-going to the point of being unconventional; derived from the mistaken belief that Bohemia was the homeland of the gipsies
a throw-off:	something discarded
monocle:	a corrective lens for one eye only
poor old Charlie Moyne:	a character who appears briefly in Part One: 3 (where no reference is made to a monocle in the description of him)
'A penny for your thoughts':	a proverbial phrase
spangles:	small, thin objects, usually metal, that glitter in light and are used to ornament women's dresses

---

Part Six: 1

Bitter and isolated, Cubitt has several drinks at a pub, wanders about the amusement area, then goes to the Cosmopolitan to offer his services to Colleoni. There Cubitt is rejected by Crab, the former ally who is now working for Colleoni (and whom Spicer met in Part Three: 3). Ida, however, befriends the lonely Cubitt, who has been left by Crab in a cocktail lounge of the hotel where Ida is having a drink. Cubitt reveals to her particulars concerning Hale's murder, reacting violently when he lets slip a reference to 'Brighton rock'. Ida rushes upstairs to fetch Phil as a witness, but on returning finds Cubitt gone. Cubitt has also told Ida that Pinkie plans to marry Rose, which intensifies Ida's desire to save the girl.

NOTES AND GLOSSARY:

Narcissus:	in Greek mythology, a beautiful youth who upon seeing his own image reflected in a spring fell in love with himself; the myth is parodied here, possibly for the second time in the novel (see earlier note for 'The Boy stood . . . shining tiles', Part Five: 1)
a splash:	soda-water added to an alcoholic drink
grey goose:	a wild goose, called a 'greylag' because it is slow to migrate from England to a warmer area

seven devils:	the evil spirits Christ cast out of Mary Magdalene; see the Bible, Luke 8:2
sibilation:	hissing sound
the seventh plane where all was very beautiful:	the seventh – and highest – heaven was thought to be the home of God and the most exalted angels
He could be . . . shake a tambourine:	during a spiritualist séance the spirits of the dead may be asked to indicate their presence in these ways
Spooner's Nook:	'to spoon' is slang for 'to make sentimental love'; thus, 'Spooner's Nook' is a secluded place (a 'nook') for innocent lovers
Amor:	(*Latin*) love
Squire's:	a squire is a country gentleman and landowner
gave you the air:	dismissed you
omen:	portent, a sign of some future, usually evil, occurrence
pomade:	a greasy, scented hair cosmetic
boule tables:	tables elaborately inlaid with, for example, brass, bronze or tortoiseshell
a Tuileries air:	Tuileries Palace was a heavily ornamented royal palace in Paris, destroyed by fire in 1871 (the Tuileries Gardens now occupy the site); a 'Tuileries air' is produced by frilly decoration
marquetry:	inlaid wood
supercilious:	contemptuously superior
Hippodrome:	a variety theatre
Havana:	the capital city of Cuba, famous for its 'Havana' cigars
salver:	serving tray
woolly:	(*figurative*) vague, hazy-minded
a courtyard . . . cock crowing:	see the Bible, Matthew 26:69–75
a diviner:	one who divines, who claims to discover truths or be able to predict the future through inspiration, guessing, intuition, or magic
gratings:	here, coverings for hot-air vents
twenty pounds:	Ida's offer to Cubitt, which she repeats to Dallow (Part Seven: 8), recalls the thirty pieces of silver for which Judas betrayed Christ (see the Bible, Matthew 26:14–15); the theme of betrayal recurs throughout *Brighton Rock*; ironically, it is Rose's loyalty to Pinkie that drives him to plot her death

Part Six: 2

Because Rose is late for the wedding, Pinkie and Dallow go for a walk to pass the time, leaving Prewitt at the registry office. To Dallow, Pinkie confides that, as a boy, he had vowed to become a priest because priests abstain from the sex act, an act he finds disgusting, even horrifying. He speaks at uncharacteristic length about the grossness of the sex act. Then, as Rose appears, Pinkie reveals that he is not listed in the municipality's register and, so far as the municipality knew, is without parents or a legal guardian. Rose explains her lateness: she had gone to church to confess, but had left before doing so because, she had felt, nothing could save her once she had consummated her relationship with Pinkie.

After a brief civil ceremony, conducted without an exchange of rings, Prewitt, Dallow, Rose, and Pinkie go to a nearby pub; there Dallow defends Rose against Pinkie's cruel words. Pinkie and Rose leave for the Cosmopolitan, where the Boy feels insulted when told that all the hotel's rooms are occupied. The two walk about to pass the time, stopping as Pinkie makes a gramophone record with a vicious message for Rose. Near, perhaps even at, the site of Hale's murder, Pinkie buys himself and Rose each a stick of Brighton rock. Then he takes her to a romantic movie. Finally, they go to Pinkie's room to spend the night, aware that, for them, sexual intercourse is an act of mortal sin because they have not been bound in holy wedlock by the Catholic Church. After Rose and Pinkie have consummated the marriage, Dallow makes an untimely appearance to collect his belongings.

Later that night Pinkie has a curious, prophetic dream, consisting of three parts: (*a*) Kite giving him a razor with which to defend himself against some school children; (*b*) himself drowning; (*c*) his parents performing their Saturday night sex act. Awakening, Pinkie takes a walk, during which he realises that only death will ever free him from Rose.

NOTES AND GLOSSARY:

Black Rock:	a rock formation on the shore east of Brighton
Film Fun:	a popular magazine for film-goers
pistils:	the female sex organs of flowers, whose seeds germinate when fertilised by pollen from stamens, the male sex organs of plants
Married Passion:	title of an invented book, presumably by one of the 'well-known sexologists' mentioned a few paragraphs above; other editions of *Brighton Rock* read '*Married Love*', one of several books by Marie Stopes (1880–1950), published in 1918, which advocated birth control as a means of enhancing

marital happiness; apparently, Greene has changed the title because the connotations of 'passion' are more suitable to the context than are those of 'love'

'What's wrong ... from this': Catholic priests take a vow of chastity

malaria: a disease caused by the bite of tropical mosquitoes, producing dangerously high fever

Annie Collins: Pinkie's description of Annie Collins's suicide is almost identical with that of a girl in Greene's childhood hometown; see the Prologue to *Lawless Roads* (1939)

the Hassocks: . a village a few miles north of Brighton

gift of tongues: ability to speak in unknown languages, which early Christians were said to have been granted by miracle; see the Bible, Acts 2

'Credo in unum Satanum': (*Latin*) 'I believe in one Satan' – a blasphemous parody of the orthodox 'credo in unum Dominum' quoted by Pinkie in Part Two: 1

tricked herself up: dressed herself up

mackintosh: a raincoat, named after the Scottish chemist Charles Macintosh (1766–1843), who invented a method of waterproofing cloth

She looked like ... an answer: this description of Rose is strikingly similar to that of the dolls at the shooting-booth (Part One: 2), which Pinkie likens to the Virgin Mary

'Roses, roses ... sprig of yew': Prewitt is apparently confusing lines of poetry from two Victorian writers: 'It was roses, roses, all the way', from Robert Browning's (1812–89) 'The Patriot'; and 'Strew on her roses, roses,/And never a spray of yew', from Matthew Arnold's (1822–88) 'Requiescat'

Nibs: metal pen-points, which here make scratching sounds as they write

the market was firm: stock-market jargon, meaning 'prices on the exchange were stable'; here used metaphorically to indicate that the marriage 'market' was stable

Extra Stout: a brand name of stout, a strong, dark English beer

tasted for the second time: in Part Five: 5 Pinkie drinks beer for the first time; his first taste of alcohol occurs in Part Five: 1, when he drinks Sylvie's cocktail

'With my body ... worldly goods': from the Solemnisation of Matrimony, The Book of Common Prayer: 'With this ring I thee wed, with my body I thee worship, and with all my worldly goods I thee endow'

gold piece: the wedding ring

swilling: pouring

yeasty cloth: a cloth smelling of yeast from the spilled beer which the cloth is used to wipe up

spittle: saliva

a married couple the image winked at him: should read 'a married couple, the image winked at him'

Margate: a popular seaside resort east of London

sloped away: went off

they felt . . . experience: Pinkie and Rose feel like Adam and Eve, who were expelled from the paradise of Eden, where they had lived in perfect, blissful innocence until they disobeyed God (the Bible, Genesis 3)

terminus: a railway station that is the last stop on a line

Pullman: a fashionable railway carriage, named after its inventor, George M. Pullman (1831–97)

pinnace: a smaller boat that attends a warship; used figuratively here to indicate the relationship of the women to the men with whom they are seen

to swank about: (*slang*) to brag about, to show off

the nocturnal act: sexual intercourse

nocturnal: of the night

penance: the willing acceptance of punishment for sin

Colleoni's gold cigarette case: in fact it was Colleoni's gold lighter that had earlier caught Pinkie's fancy (Part Two: 2)

wicker chairs: chairs made of plaited twigs (wickers)

Stickphast: a brand of glue

He'd eat a packet of chocolate: yet in Part One: 2 Pinkie asserts that he does not eat chocolates

anglers: fishermen who use a hook and line

floats: a float is a piece of buoyant material, such as cork, attached to a fishing line; a fish taking the bait causes the buoyant material to bob, which indicates a bite to the fisherman

paraphernalia: equipment

vulcanite: hard, black rubber that has been vulcanised to make it durable and thereby suitable for making gramophone records (see earlier note for 'the vulcanite', Part Three: 2)

ghost train: an amusement park ride in which participants ride in a sort of roller coaster through a dark tunnel, where ghosts, skeletons, and other mechanical contrivances designed to frighten spring out unexpectedly, with suitable accompanying noises

Magpie Ices:	a commercial name for a brand of ice-cream
Photoweigh:	a combined photograph booth and weighing machine
Rocko:	presumably the name of a shop selling Brighton rock, brightly coloured candy sticks
winkles:	periwinkles – small, edible sea snails
Eucharist:	the central Christian sacrament, in which the worshipper is united with Christ by partaking of consecrated bread and wine which symbolise His body and blood
coracles:	a coracle is a primitive type of small boat which has a woven grass or sapling frame covered with hide or other waterproof material
Santa Monica:	a California seaside resort in Los Angeles County
absolution:	forgiveness of sins by an ecclesiastical authority
contrition:	overwhelming regret and sorrow for sin
Garbo cheeks:	the Swedish film actress Greta Garbo (*b.*1905) has extremely prominent high cheek bones
untenanted:	not occupied by a rent-payer, a tenant
'Two's company':	(*proverbial*) 'two's company, three's a crowd'
bugger:	(*vulgar*) term of abuse for a man
This was hell then:	although Pinkie is clearly no reader of Elizabethan drama, these words are perhaps meant to emphasise the Boy's demonic nature by recalling Mephistopheles's acknowledgement that he carries his own hell about with him wherever he goes: 'Why this is hell, nor am I out of it'; from Christopher Marlowe's (1564–93) *Doctor Faustus*, I.3.80; in Part Seven: 3 Prewitt quotes the line, changing 'I' to 'we'
It was as if . . . any night:	'He [the Romantic poet John Keats (1795–1821)] has out-soared the shadow of the night'; from Percy Bysshe Shelley's (1792–1822) pastoral elegy, *Adonais*; Pinkie improbably compares his newly sexually initiated self to an artistic idealist who in death transcended the baser elements of mortal life
eggshell:	an emblem of innocence: Pinkie had thought Rose to be as innocent as a newly hatched chick
the piece of gold . . . the blessing:	a reference to the Catholic wedding ceremony; the 'piece of gold in the palm' is the wedding ring
purgatory:	according to Roman Catholic doctrine souls who die in a state of grace must expiate their sins in purgatory before entering heaven

phosphorescent: shining without an apparent source
'Blessed art thou among women': the angel Gabriel's words to the Virgin Mary at the Annunciation (see the Bible, Luke 1:28)

Part Seven: 1

Rose awakens in Pinkie's room in the boarding-house to find the Boy gone. Exploring the kitchen, she meets Dallow searching for Judy, his mistress and the wife of Frank, a blind man who runs a dry-cleaning business and owns the boarding-house. Dallow tells Rose not to worry about doing any housework, then continues looking for Judy. Shortly afterwards Rose comes across Dallow and Judy embracing passionately. Dallow introduces the two women to each other, and Judy asks Rose not to tell Frank about her and Dallow's affair. Proud of her newly acquired experience, Rose goes to Snow's, where she talks to one of the waitresses. On her way back, hearing a gramophone in a shop close to Frank's, she asks permission to play her record of Pinkie's voice sometime. In Pinkie's room Rose finds Ida, who has gained admittance to the room by posing as Rose's mother. Ida wants Rose to give evidence against Pinkie, but Rose is steadfast. Ida informs Rose that her life is in danger and, as she leaves, warns the girl about becoming pregnant by a murderer. Rose, however, is delighted by the prospect of becoming the mother of Pinkie's child.

NOTES AND GLOSSARY:

dinned: urged noisily
'Our Fathers' and 'Hail Marys': prayers to God and to the Virgin Mary
coke: a type of heating fuel made from coal
Liberty Hall: a place where one may do what one likes: a phrase from Oliver Goldsmith's (1728–74) comedy *She Stoops to Conquer*, Act II
routing: poking around, moving about aimlessly
prehensile: grasping
sea anemone: a sea animal that attaches itself to, for example, rocks
conscripted: forced to enlist for state service, usually military
duck: (*colloquial*) dear, darling
hubby: (*colloquial*) husband
russet: reddish-brown
esoteric: understandable only to the initiated
eight-thirty Matins: a non-Eucharistic morning service of the Anglican Church, that is, a service not involving the worshipper with Christ through the partaking of consecrated bread and wine (see earlier note for 'Eucharist', Part Six: 2)

coppers:	(*slang*) pennies and halfpennies; so-called because these coins were formerly made of copper
***News of the World*:**	a sensationalistic Sunday newspaper published in London since 1843
gaol:	jail
'I don't want to let the Innocent suffer':	see earlier note for 'I don't want the Innocent to suffer', Part Four: 2
aphorism:	short, memorable statement of a general principle
a God wept . . . a cross:	biblical reference to Christ's agony in the Garden of Gethsemane and to His cry on the cross, 'My God, my God, why hast thou forsaken me?' (see the Bible, Matthew 26 and 27)

Part Seven: 2

Pinkie returns to his room, increasingly distrustful of Rose despite Dallow's faith in her loyalty. He questions Rose about Ida's visits, then conceives a plan to get rid of her by means of a double suicide, intending only to fake his part of the deal. Rose agrees to the suicide pact.

NOTES AND GLOSSARY:

Epping Forest:	a forest north-east of London
the whole bloody boiling:	(*slang*) the whole damned lot; from 'boiling' in reference to a large amount of vegetables boiled together
toecap:	leather covering of the toe of a shoe
straight:	honest, loyal
stuck on:	(*slang*) in love with
seven devils:	see earlier note for 'seven devils', Part Six: 1
the Soul of Honour:	used ironically here: as a lawyer Prewitt ought to be an honourable man, but due to his own weaknesses he has been corrupted by Pinkie

---

Part Seven: 3

Pinkie calls on Prewitt, who the Boy fears will break under Ida's pressure. Pained by a stomach ulcer and slightly drunk, Prewitt tells Pinkie, who is astonished at these self-revelations, about his ruined life. Then Pinkie bribes him into leaving England for France.

NOTES AND GLOSSARY:

shunting engines:	railway engines switching to side tracks
cavalier:	courtly gentlman
'Eat, drink, for tomorrow . . .':	'Let us eat and drink, for tomorrow we shall die' (the Bible, Isaiah 22:13)

'How now? A rat?': from Shakespeare's *Hamlet*, III.4.23; the words are
    spoken by Hamlet about Polonius
'What ho! old mole': 'Well said, old mole! canst work i' the earth so fast?';
    Hamlet, I.5.162

A swell:	(*slang*) an expert
gasometers:	a gasometer is a storage tank for gas
bonhomie:	joviality

'Why, this ... of it': see note for 'This was hell then', Part Six: 2
To pull down . . . like Samson: see the biblical story of Samson in Judges,
    especially 16:25–31; see also the note below for the
    allusion to Milton's *Samson Agonistes* (Part Seven:
    6)

Lancaster:	town in Lancashire in north-west England

Public Schools Year Book: a year book listing recognised public (i.e.
    privately run, independent) schools

Harrow:	one of England's best-known public schools
esprit de corps:	(*French*) team spirit
cellarage:	cellar, basement
Head:	a headmaster, or head, is a school's chief figure of authority
grubby:	dirty, grimy

'I have done the state some service': 'I have done the state some service,
    and they know't'; Shakespeare's *Othello*, V.2.338

leech:	a blood-sucking worm
villa:	a detached or semi-detached house with a small garden

Part Seven: 4

Back at Frank's, Pinkie is irritated to find that Rose has cleaned and
tidied his room. He repeats to her his scheme of a double suicide. Deeply
touched by the sound of a child crying next door, Rose suggests to Pinkie
that she might herself have a child by him – a possibility that both
terrifies and disgusts the Boy.

NOTES AND GLOSSARY:

wireless masts:	posts or poles, on the tops of which are radio ('wireless') aerials
rivet:	a type of bolt

Part Seven: 5

By the next morning the troubled, restless Pinkie is convinced that he
must carry out his double suicide plot and so rid himself of Rose.

Dallow, anxiously awaiting news of Prewitt's departure for France,
again tries to convince Pinkie of the girl's loyalty. Pinkie reveals that,
when he was alone and ill in the cold, the gang's former leader, Kite, had
taken him in and that he has himself picked up several of Kite's personal
eccentricities. Dallow reads the Boy a letter from Colleoni offering
Pinkie three hundred pounds if he will abandon the race-track
protection racket. A phone call from a comrade, Johnnie, confirms that
Prewitt is now on a boat to France.

NOTES AND GLOSSARY:

the vulcanite:	the hard, black rubber of the telephone (see earlier note for 'the vulcanite', Part Three: 2)
in a shake:	(*slang*) in a moment
bales:	large bundles of merchandise that have been wrapped and tied
ascetic:	denying all sensual pleasures
Pekinese:	an expensive breed of toy pug dog, developed in ancient China (hence the name: 'inhabitant of Peking'); the dog has short legs, a flat face, and long hair
suckers:	(*slang*) here, those foolish enough to bet on horses at the race-track
Leicester:	a Midlands (central England) industrial town in Leicestershire
Goodwood:	a village to the west of Brighton; it has a famous race-track
Hurst Park:	the site of another race-course, now defunct
Newmarket:	a town north of London long famous for horse breeding, and the home of the Jockey Club
coition:	sexual intercourse
vexed:	irritated, angered
smooth:	(*figurative*) unruffled
boar's:	a boar is a male pig that has not been castrated

Part Seven: 6

In the same tea-room in which Pinkie's mob met in Part One: 2 after
murdering Hale, Ida and Phil see Pinkie, Rose, Dallow and Judy sitting
several tables away from them. To Phil, who wants to turn the case over
to the police, Ida confirms that her tenacious pursuit of the Boy will not
stop until Rose is safe.

NOTES AND GLOSSARY:

arms:	coat of arms: here, the badge or shield of the organisation whose blazer Phil is wearing

all passion spent:	an ironic reference to the well-known closing lines of John Milton's (1608–74) closet drama, *Samson Agonistes*: 'His [God's] servants he with new acquist,/Of true experience from this great event,/With peace and consolation hath dismiss'd,/And calm of mind, all passion spent'; the sexually inadequate Phil is being playfully compared with Milton's mighty hero, who, though weakened by contact with a woman, eventually arose to destroy the Philistines at God's command (see earlier note for 'To pull down . . . like Samson', Part Seven: 3)
'It's fate':	the ancient Greeks – with whom Ida is associated (see earlier note for 'Ida', Part One: 1) – believed that the Fates prescribed at birth one's destined lot in life; thus, not only is the Catholic Pinkie doomed to fall spiritually because he is a sinner, he is also fated to be punished physically because he is a criminal
with your money:	yet it is not clear when Ida paid Cubitt
fernery:	a place for growing ferns, plants with feathery leaves
Worthing:	a seaside resort west of Brighton
punchball:	an inflated ball, suspended from a frame, which a boxer punches rhythmically as a form of training
tipsily:	slightly drunkenly

Part Seven: 7

When Pinkie sees Ida laughing in the tea-room, he feels defeated and leaves with Rose. Dropping information to bystanders that he plans to use later for alibi purposes, Pinkie guides Rose to his car and drives her out into the countryside to carry out the suicide pact. On the way Rose is attracted by a little girl pressing her face against the window of a bus passing Pinkie's Morris. Pinkie and Rose stop at a hotel, ostensibly for drinks, but really so that the Boy can establish another alibi. They are served by Piker, whom Pinkie used to bully at school. Pinkie tells Rose to write a suicide note, then goes to the men's room, where he loads his revolver.

NOTES AND GLOSSARY:

arterials:	see earlier note for 'arterial road', Part Five: 1
charabancs:	from *char à bancs* (*French*), sightseeing buses
ferret:	a half-tamed polecat used for hunting rabbits
the Down:	the treeless chalk hills of southern England; called 'the downs' in Part Three: 3

get your rag out: (*slang*) become angry
the bull: the bull's-eye, the centre of a target
an outer: a target circle outside the bull's-eye
pedantically: with great concern for detail
the darkest nightmare of all: the phrase – and its context – anticipates the novel's ending
the rent: the tear, referring to the torn top of Pinkie's Morris, mentioned in Part One: 1
cataract: an eye disease causing eventual blindness
intone: recite in a chant-like manner
the dying man in the St Pancras waiting-room: Kite; see earlier note for 'Who was Kite? . . . St Pancras', Part Three: 1
pipe-dream: fantasy; from the hallucinatory dreams opium-pipe smokers experience
cutting: excavation
go into that darkness: die
Lureland: perhaps the name of a dance-hall
Whist Drive: a card-playing competition (whist is a card game)
dado: a frieze or border round the walls of a room
Tudor roses: the red rose was the emblem of the house of Lancaster, which produced the Tudor monarchs (reigned 1485–1603)
Siphons: siphon-bottles, which dispense soda water for drinks by gas-pressure
breaks: short periods of recess between school classes
atmospherics: static – crackling sounds on a radio caused by electrical disturbances in the atmosphere
Moorish-Tudor-God-knows-what-of-a-lamp: the lamp mingles at least two incompatible styles, the Tudor (English Renaissance) and the Moorish (Islamic Medieval)
'Holy Mary, Mother of God': the opening words of a prayer
depression: a lowering of atmospheric pressure
chaplet: a wreath

Part Seven: 8

Back in the tea-room, Ida persuades Dallow to confide in her, frightening him with the false information that Prewitt is in the custody of the police. Convinced that Pinkie might be planning something that endangers Rose's life, Ida forces Dallow to hire a car by threatening to implicate him in Rose's murder. Ida and Dallow then set out to follow Pinkie's trail.

NOTES AND GLOSSARY:
mooning: gazing dreamily

cumbrously:	clumsily
solicitors:	a solicitor is a type of lawyer
quay:	pier, wharf: a landing place for ships
barnacled:	(*figurative*) covered; a barnacle is a sea crustacean that attaches itself to the bottom of ships and to rocks
to have a drain:	(*slang*) to urinate
pitch on:	choose, select
crackers:	(*slang*) crazy
gammy:	(*slang*) game: crippled, lame

Part Seven: 9

In the meantime, at the road-house two vulgar upper-class men laugh at Rose's lack of sexual attractiveness. Rose gives Pinkie the suicide note he had asked her to write. When she affirms that she will stick by him always, Pinkie knows that only through death will he ever be rid of her and decides irrevocably to go through with the false double-suicide scheme. Accordingly, the two drive to the place Pinkie has selected for Rose's suicide. However, as Rose prepares to shoot herself in the head with Pinkie's revolver, Ida arrives on the scene with Dallow and a policeman. Just as Rose is about to pull the trigger, she hears Pinkie's name called out and, taking this as a good omen, throws the gun away. Pinkie pulls out his bottle of vitriol to throw at Dallow as a punishment for betraying him; but the policeman, breaking the bottle with his baton, sends the vitriol spraying into Pinkie's face. Howling with pain, burnt by his own vitriol, the Boy turns, runs towards the edge of the cliff close by, and hurls himself over and into the sea.

NOTES AND GLOSSARY:

gambits:	strategies; from the chess term 'gambit', an opening move in which a pawn is sacrificed to gain advantage
swagger:	here, a conceited glance
sting:	(*slang*) charge money, with the implication of an excessive amount
hot:	(*figurative*) sexually passionate
cane:	the stem of certain plants used for punishment by whipping
havoc:	disorder, chaos
confession:	admission to a priest, in private, of one's sins
sacrament:	the Eucharist, the Holy Communion in the Catholic Church uniting the partaker with Christ (see earlier note for 'Eucharist', Part Six: 2)

the laughing Cavalier: famous painting by the Dutch artist Frans Hals
      (?1580–1666); it hangs in the Wallace Collection,
      London

'He was in . . . Him not': see the Bible, John 17

to fight in Spain: the Spanish Civil War (1936–9) attracted many
      adventurous young men from other countries

the crib at Christmas: actually, at birth the Christ child was placed in a
      straw-lined manger (a feeding trough for cattle and
      horses) because Mary and Joseph, His parents, had
      no crib; the nativity scene is a familiar motif for
      Christmas decorations

Herod seeking . . . turreted keep: see the Bible, Matthew 2

the scalping knife or the bayonet wound: in frontier days, as an emblem of
      victory some American Indians cut off the scalps of
      their enemies; soldiers often attach knives (bayonets)
      to their rifle muzzles for stabbing enemy troops

guardian angel: a protective religious spirit

instructions: religious teachings

scrub: shrubbery

deputation: group of persons appointed to represent someone

squealer: (*slang*) one who has informed against another

badgered: teased, pestered

Part Seven: 10

On her return to her home town, London, Ida relates her adventures to
Clarence at Henekey's bar. These events, Ida says, have occurred during
the past week or two, between the time she went back down to Brighton
to bet on Black Boy and pursue Pinkie (Part Three: 1), and Pinkie's
death (Part Seven: 9). Ida reveals that she has taken Rose back to the
Wilson home in Nelson Place. When Ida returns to her room, she finds
waiting for her a letter from Tom, her husband, from whom she is
estranged, asking her to take him back. She decides to consult the
planchette on whether or not she should respond favourably to his wish.

NOTES AND GLOSSARY:

barrel: a cask for storing beer or wine; see the first
      paragraph of Part One: 3

'I couldn't chase over France for him': it is unclear how Ida learned or
      deduced that Prewitt was going to France

slander: a false statement, made orally, damaging to a
      person's character

figurehead: ornamental carved figure of symbolic value, on the
      bow of a ship

char: charwoman, or woman cleaner
It was like ... accustomed rails: the movement of Ida's mind to
                           commonplace slogans is similar to a railway engine
                           switching to a familiar track
there's more things in heaven and earth ...: words from Shakespeare that
                           have passed into the popular idiom: 'There are more
                           things in heaven and earth, Horatio/Than are
                           dreamt of in' your philosophy' (*Hamlet*, I.5.166–7)

Part Seven: 11

In a confessional booth Rose claims that she wants to be damned, like
Pinkie. But the priest suggests that, God's ways being inscrutable,
Pinkie may in the end have been saved. If the Boy loved her, the priest
continues, even in his own perverse way, then there was goodness in him.
Proudly convinced that she is pregnant, Rose heads for Frank's to
retrieve her recording of Pinkie's wicked message, which will invalidate
the priest's consoling words and so prove for her the 'worst horror of
all'.

NOTES AND GLOSSARY:
eucalyptus: the strong-smelling oil of the leaves of the
                           eucalyptus tree is used as a medicine for respiratory
                           illnesses
absolution: formal forgiveness of sins by a priest
'There was a man ... the war': Charles Péguy (1873–1914), French poet
                           and essayist whose interest in the connection
                           between common daily life and the world of the
                           spirit greatly influenced Greene; however, as the
                           priest says, for Péguy – unlike for Pinkie, whom the
                           priest is comparing to Péguy – damnation was
                           sacrificial
'greater love ... his friend': 'Greater love hath no man than this, that a
                           man lay down his life for his friends' (the Bible,
                           John 15:13)
'*Corruptio optimi est pessima*': (*Latin*) 'The corruption of the best is the
                           worst'

Part 3

Commentary

Greene's Introduction to *Brighton Rock*

In 1970 – nearly a quarter-century after he had written *Brighton Rock* – Greene wrote a retrospective Introduction to the Collected Edition of the novel. This contains: (1) general comments on religion and novel writing; and (2) more specific comments on *Brighton Rock*.

(1) About the relationship of religion to his occupation as a novelist Greene says:
    (*a*) He is not a Catholic novelist, but a novelist who is a Catholic – that is, Catholicism is a part of the texture of his art, rather than his art being a vehicle for his Catholicism.
    (*b*) Although widely read in the literature of theology, he did not, until *Brighton Rock*, incorporate theology into his fiction.
    (*c*) Two historical events contemporary with the writing of *Brighton Rock* – the Spanish Civil War and the persecution of Catholics in Mexico – caused him to bring religion into his novels.

(2) About *Brighton Rock* Greene says:
    (*a*) He had begun *Brighton Rock* as a detective novel, but had found himself injecting religious material in a manner he now feels to be overly obvious.
    (*b*) Part One ought to be removed – the novel should have been rewritten so that it could begin with Part Two.
    (*c*) Much of the novel's Brighton setting does, or at one time did, exist; but much of it is also invented.
    (*d*) The real-life city of Brighton is actually associated for him with high romance, and not with the violence infesting his fictional Brighton.
    (*e*) Pinkie's lawyer, Prewitt, is the only character based on an actual person he remembered from visiting Brighton.

Approaches to *Brighton Rock*

There is no single agreed interpretation of *Brighton Rock*, nor even agreement about such central matters as whether Pinkie is a hero or a villain. Although each reader must arrive at an interpretation that he himself finds convincing, the following readings of *Brighton Rock* suggest several possible approaches – not all of them compatible with one another. These approaches highlight those aspects of the novel that have produced critical controversy and uncertainty.

Brighton Rock as a detective story

The 'thriller' elements of *Brighton Rock* – the violent, rapidly paced action – are shaped by the conventions of the detective story, a tale in which detection is used to solve a mysterious crime, usually murder. Edgar Allan Poe (1809–49) is generally agreed to have invented the genre with 'The Murders in the Rue Morgue' (1841). It is possible to distinguish two types of detective story: (*a*) the 'whodunit', a crime story whose point is the discovery of who committed the crime in question ('The Murders in the Rue Morgue' is an example); and (*b*) a tale focusing on the methods by which the criminal is caught (Poe's 'The Purloined Letter' (1845) is probably the first such story).

In Poe's detective stories may be identified the essential ingredients found in virtually all later tales of detection. Correspondingly, several of these ingredients are used in *Brighton Rock*: (*a*) the apparently perfect crime (Hale's murder is officially listed as a natural death); (*b*) the bungling police (Brighton's police inspector dismisses Ida's suspicions about Hale's death, and a policeman contributes to Pinkie's end only because Ida tricks a confused officer into coming with her); (*c*) the ineffectual companion who emphasises the detective's gifts (the timid Phil Corkery underlines Ida's tenacity and, when he does not see the significance Ida perceives in Rose's lie that 'Kolley Kibber' ordered Bass, her powers of deduction); (*d*) the eccentric amateur detective (Ida is a casual bar-room entertainer who drinks with gusto while she investigates, sings sentimental ballads, mothers those from whom she seeks leads, and trusts to the messages her planchette provides); (*e*) a dénouement, or unravelling of the plot, in which the detective explains his methods (Part Seven: 10).

To these ingredients modern detective stories have added a few characteristics of their own, for example, a psychological approach, in which crime and detection are seen to symbolise a deeper reality (see pp. 5–6 above, 'Greene's fiction'). Secondly, recent tales of detection often show an increased interest in the criminal. (Pinkie receives more narrative space than Ida.) Finally, modern detective writers seek a heightened realism, trying to capture the authentic atmosphere of the underworld and to create detectives who are more believable than such earlier sleuths as Sir Arthur Conan Doyle's (1859–1930) famous Sherlock Holmes, whose character traits are limited to those necessary for his detective work – he has, for instance, no interest in or need of such basic human emotions as love. (Greene spends considerable time depicting both the squalor surrounding Pinkie's low-grade mob and the luxury achieved by Colleoni's successful gang; and Ida is surely the earthiest detective in English literature.)

Because of the the greater focus on the criminal and the intensified realism, modern detective fiction, including *Brighton Rock*, is frequently written in the so-called 'hard-boiled', or 'tough', style, as opposed to the formal, drawing-room English used by such predecessors as the stories of Poe and Conan Doyle. The narrative of *Brighton Rock* is, generally, rendered in simple, informal language that is fairly close to spoken English – common, everyday words, such colloquial features as contractions, and conventional syntax. The imagery is seldom elaborate, puzzling or cryptic, but is drawn, instead, from familiar sources (the dominant images are of school, warfare, religion and disease). Greene avoids persistent use of literary allusions (except as a means of characterising Prewitt). Moreover, structurally, the novel moves in a straight line, from the event that incites the action, Hale's murder, to the death of Hale's murderer. There are few flashbacks or other switches of chronology as tension mounts linearly because of Pinkie's increasing desperation and dependence on violence. All these features are suitable for Greene's remorseless tale of the fall of a cut-throat teenage leader of a small-time race-track mob.

However, no critic would stop in his analysis of *Brighton Rock* after considering only its detective-story framework. To do this would be to reduce the meaning of the whole to that of one of its parts. An interpretation that ignores other aspects, especially the religious, must surely miss the novel's substance.

Brighton Rock as a religious novel

Greene has been labelled a 'Christian tragedian' by one critic, and the numerous religious references – biblical allusions, quotations from the Catholic Mass, frequently recurring terms such as 'mercy', 'sin', and 'pride' – indicate that religion is central to the meaning of *Brighton Rock*. One religious reading sees the novel as a medieval allegory, with Pinkie representing evil, Rose goodness, and Ida humanity. Another interpretation views *Brighton Rock* as part of a virtual trilogy: it deals with hell, *The Heart of the Matter* (1948) with purgatory, and *The Power and the Glory* (1940) with heaven.

On the surface – the 'entertainment' level – *Brighton Rock* seems straightforward enough: Pinkie commits the crime of murder and is hunted down for it, and in the end justice is done. But the deeper, more serious level – the level at which religion is central – is more difficult to interpret. In committing his crime, Pinkie is guilty of religious sin (murder violates the sixth of the Bible's Ten Commandments). Pinkie is also hunted down spiritually by the lack of inner peace (the word recurs again and again) resulting from Ida's dogged pursuit of him, until death seems to him the only restful state.

But is Pinkie finally damned or saved? Certainly his sins seem to be numerous enough and serious enough to warrant his damnation, and Rose believes that Pinkie is finally damned. Indeed, although Pinkie holds scant belief in heaven, his convictions about the 'Flames', 'damnation', and 'torments' of hell are strong: 'Heaven was a word: Hell was something he could trust' (Part Seven: 7). Moreover, because of such ideas, Pinkie is guilty of religious despair, the belief that God will not grant him salvation. This is the eighth and most deadly sin because the despairing soul denies the saving mercy of God's grace. And Pinkie expresses his despair by committing suicide, for a Catholic the worst possible act.

Yet at the very end of the novel the priest tells Rose of the inconceivable, 'appalling . . . strangeness of the mercy of God' (Part Seven: 11; Greene's ellipsis). That is, because God's granting of salvation transcends mortal comprehension, it can never be known whether God has extended His grace to the Boy or not, no matter how damnable Pinkie is by mortal standards. Further, running throughout the novel is the motto 'Between the stirrup and the ground, he mercy sought and mercy found.' In other words, so long as one repents before dying, the doors of salvation are open. Now precisely what happens in *Brighton Rock* is that Pinkie *falls* to his death; but, because Greene narrates Pinkie's death from the point of view of Rose, the reader never learns whether or not Pinkie repents 'between the stirrup and the ground' – that is, between the time he leaps from the cliff and when he hits the water below and drowns. And toward the end, the Boy's evil impulses are checked momentarily by 'An enormous emotion [that] beat on him; it was like something trying to get in; the pressure of gigantic wings against the glass. Dona nobis pacem . . . . If the glass broke, if the beast – whatever it was – got in, God knows what it would do. He had a sense of huge havoc – the confession, the penance and the sacrament – and awful distraction' (Part Seven: 9). Greene, then, has left at least the possibility of Pinkie's salvation open, and he has clearly manipulated the narrative to disallow the reader final insight into Pinkie's last thoughts.

Brighton Rock as an existentialist novel

As opposed to looking at the novel as an age-old tale of sin and damnation, some readers have considered *Brighton Rock* from the perspective of modern existentialism, a philosophy holding, in general, that man is free and responsible for developing his own character through acts of will. 'Existentialism' is, however, an uncomfortably loose term to try to apply in any systematic way to literary works (other than those written by professed existentialists): the questions of whose existentialism is being used as a point of reference, and what the term really means, are unavoidable.

Generally, the critical technique used in existentialist readings of *Brighton Rock* is to select an idea from existentialist philosophy, then to point out the recurrence of that idea in the fiction. The existentialist idea most frequently applied to *Brighton Rock* is that each person's character is of his own making; he has complete freedom to do what he will and what he can with his life. Accordingly, Rose has been considered to be an existentialist heroine because she projects a meaningful future for herself as the potential mother of Pinkie's child. And Pinkie has been similarly labelled an existentialist because, in choosing freely to damn himself, he forges his own identity, even if it is a negative one.

In evaluating these interpretations, the reader of *Brighton Rock* would do well to keep several points in mind. In the case of Rose, for example, (a) there is no proof that she is pregnant; and (b) what is certain is that what she considers to be the 'darkest nightmare of all' – that Pinkie does not love her – is precisely what she is about to experience as the novel closes. If she is not pregnant, then the crucial source of her new identity is negated; and if Rose is pregnant, then her discovery that Pinkie actually hated her will be even more shattering. As for Pinkie, it is difficult to argue that his decision to go to hell is a heroic one with which the reader is meant to sympathise; not only does the overall tone of the story suggest otherwise, but textual support for such an interpretation is lacking. Pinkie's suicide, for instance, is rendered in a manner that is clearly not heroic: as Pinkie races for the edge of the cliff, he looks 'half his size – and he shrank – shrank into a schoolboy flying in panic and pain' (Part Seven: 9). The meaninglessness of his death is emphasised by the fact that none of the other characters hears the splash his body makes as it hits the water. The sum total of this insignificant life is 'zero – nothing' (Part Seven: 9).

Brighton Rock as a naturalistic novel

Perhaps somewhat more convincing than an existentialist explanation is an interpretation of *Brighton Rock* as a naturalistic novel, that is, a story in which the characters' fates are determined by biological and environmental forces over which the characters themselves have no control. Such a reading actually contradicts an existentialist interpretation; as the protagonist's fate in a naturalistic novel is determined by forces outside himself, he lacks free will, a distinguishing trait of the existentialist hero.

Pinkie himself ascribes to biology his seemingly innate predilection for evil: 'It's in the blood', he tells Rose (Part Four: 3). Further, Pinkie's environment has helped to shape his character. Products of the crushing poverty of Paradise Piece, Pinkie's 'cells were formed of the cement playground, the dead fire and the dying man [Kite] in the St Pancras waiting room, his bed at Frank's and his parents' bed' (Part Seven: 7). To Pinkie, this unfortunate background justifies his dedication to crime: surveying Rose's impoverished home, the Boy believes that he could not be blamed for committing criminal acts which raise him above such a life.

Before accepting this interpretation, however, the reader should consider that (*a*) the naturalistic elements form only a few paragraphs of the whole novel; (*b*) the biological interpretation of Pinkie's evil can just as well be attributed to the theological doctrine of Original Sin (the belief that Adam and Eve's disobedience of God in the Garden of Eden tainted all future generations); (*c*) Rose, certainly a more sympathetic character than Pinkie, whom the Boy several times acknowledges to be his polar opposite, 'goodness', comes from an environment virtually identical to Pinkie's – that is, although Pinkie and Rose are products of a 'common geography' (Part Three: 3), their established characters are divergent; (*d*) at least two components of naturalism, the irrelevancy or non-existence of God and the presentation of a great number of descriptive details, are missing from *Brighton Rock*.

Brighton Rock as a psychological novel

Occasionally principles of theoretical psychology can be used as frameworks within which to interpret literary texts. For instance, Pinkie's sexual aberrations can be understood as a form of sublimation (the re-channelling of drives that cannot find normal expression). According to Sigmund Freud (1856–1939), the founder of psychoanalysis, sexual energy that is thwarted can be redirected toward socially acceptable ends. Pinkie, however, unable to realise his sexual impulses in a healthy manner because of the traumatic Saturday-night sexual ritual his parents performed in front of him every week when he was a child, sublimates his sexual energy, not into socially approved activities, but into sadism (the attainment of sexual gratification through cruelty). For him the 'finest of all sensations [is] the infliction of pain' (Part Four: 1). Consequently, loving by means of hatred, Pinkie expresses his sexuality through violence. As he fingers the bottle of vitriol in his pocket, for example, he feels a 'faint secret sexual pleasure', which is 'his nearest approach to passion' (Part Two: 1). Later, 'His fingers curled with passionate hatred round the small bottle' (Part Five: 2). As he pinches Rose's wrist, Pinkie works 'himself into a little sensual rage'

(Part Two: 1). At one point Pinkie begins pulling off the legs and wings of an insect one at a time: 'She loves me', he says, 'she loves me not. I've been out with my girl, Spicer' (Part Three: 4). And as he guides the unwitting Spicer towards Colleoni's waiting mob, Pinkie feels 'cruelty straightening his body like lust'; 'A passion of cruelty stirred in his belly'. After escaping from Colleoni's men, Pinkie walks past a couple embracing 'with his cruel virginity which demanded some satisfaction different from theirs, habitual, brutish and short'. And when Rose lifts her face for the Boy to kiss her, Pinkie wants 'to strike her, to make her scream' (Part Four: 1). Finally, again with Rose, Pinkie's putting a finger-nail on her cheek is 'half caress, half threat' (Part Seven: 9). When Pinkie does have intercourse with Rose, he does so violently, 'in a kind of rage . . . he pushed her against the bed . . . he blotted everything out in a sad brutal now-or-never embrace' (Part Six: 2). Ironically, as a child Pinkie had wanted to sublimate his sexuality into one of the most socially acceptable of all vocations, the priesthood. He reveals this intention to Dallow after describing how he had witnessed his parents' regular Saturday night 'bouncing and ploughing'; Pinkie's 'eyes flinched as if he were watching some horror'. The priesthood, then, attracted Pinkie because, being celibate, priests 'keep away' from the 'horror' of sex (Part Six: 2).

Other aspects of *Brighton Rock* that can be considered from a psychological viewpoint include Pinkie's obsessive puritanism – besides being unable to enjoy music, Pinkie refuses to drink, smoke, gamble, dance, and of course, before Rose, have anything to do with girls. The reader might also consider the Boy's dream in Part Six: 2, especially in the light of the earlier observation that Pinkie's is a dreamless, purely 'functional' sleep. Finally, that Kite, the mob's previous leader, is a father-figure to Pinkie is implied several times. Similarly, Ida once imagines herself to be Pinkie's mother and is in turn once imagined by Pinkie to be his mother; and at one point she successfully misrepresents herself as Rose's mother and, hence, as Pinkie's mother-in-law.

In applying psychology to literature, however, it is crucial to avoid over-schematising a work by forcing it into a preconceived framework. For instance, it may at first be tempting to analyse *Brighton Rock* in terms of Freud's three-tiered personality structure consisting of the id – the unconscious, impulsive drives (Pinkie); the super-ego – the censor of the id (Rose); and the ego – the reality principle, which seeks to reconcile the demands of the id to the moral codes of the super-ego (Ida). However, this formula can probably only be applied to *Brighton Rock* by greatly distorting the major lines of the novel.

Point of view in *Brighton Rock*

In fiction, 'point of view' refers to the perspective from which the reader receives the narrative. Eighteenth- and nineteenth-century novels are usually related by an all-seeing, all-knowing 'omniscient' narrator capable of entering the mind of each character and of commenting, even moralising, on the action. More recent fiction is often narrated from a viewpoint limited to that of one or more characters, so that the reader learns only what a particular character knows, remembers, thinks or experiences. Often a writer will combine these two techniques, rendering part of his story from an omniscient point of view and the rest from the point of view of one or more specific characters.

Such a combination of points of view is Greene's method in *Brighton Rock*. Pinkie's death, for instance, achieves heightened dramatic impact by being narrated from Rose's perspective because the reader, sharing Rose's mortal limitations, never learns whether or not in the end God extends to Pinkie His inscrutable mercy. And a few pages later, Greene closes the novel from the omniscient point of view, creating a tantalising ending in which Rose decides to play the record that contains, as the all-knowing narrator puts it, the 'worst horror of all' – Pinkie's cruel message, of which the innocent, loving Rose is sadly ignorant (Part Seven: 11).

Another skilful use of point of view in *Brighton Rock* is the handling of the first section of Part One, in which the frantic Hale tries desperately to avoid Pinkie's mob and at the same time to carry out his job as 'Kolley Kibber'. Except for the last paragraph, this episode is restricted to Hale's viewpoint, which creates immediate tension by involving the reader directly in Hale's precarious situation. The last paragraph, however, shifts, unobtrusively, to Ida's perspective as she goes into the lavatory to wash, emerging to find that Hale has disappeared. Ample suggestions of Hale's fate have been provided to allow the reader to imagine a confrontation between Hale and the mob that, like the off-stage violence in Shakespeare's plays, is probably more effective dramatically than an actual depiction of Hale's kidnapping and murder would be. Further, Ida, unaware of Hale's fate, puts a naively innocent interpretation on Hale's disappearance, ironically heightening the tension, rather than lowering it, and creating an effective contrast with the following section, which is told from the point of view of the guilty Pinkie.

Some inconsistencies do, however, occur in the point of view of *Brighton Rock*. For example, in an episode clearly related from Pinkie's perspective, Pinkie, contemplating death, remembers several specific details concerning Kite's murder at St Pancras railway station in London. Pinkie recalls Kite 'passing out in the waiting-room, while a porter poured coal-dust on the dead grate, talking all the time about someone's tits' (Part Four: 1), even though apparently neither the Boy, nor any other member of the mob, was present (as no one seems to have assisted Kite, the context implies that he was alone; and besides, except to visit a few race-tracks, Pinkie has never left Brighton, according to what he tells Dallow toward the end of the novel).

Characterisation

The novel's three main characters, Pinkie, Rose, and Ida, can be considered in two groups: (*a*) Pinkie and Rose; (*b*) Ida. Of the minor characters in *Brighton Rock*, Spicer, Cubitt, Dallow and Prewitt are allies of Pinkie; Colleoni opposes the Boy; Phil is associated with Ida; and Hale with both Pinkie and Ida.

Major characters

Throughout *Brighton Rock*, Pinkie and Rose are portrayed as doubles: mirror images at once identical and also contrastive. Their thinness of body and immature, generally childlike physical appearance are repeatedly mentioned, emphasising their similarity. Both are Roman Catholics from lower-class neighbourhoods. Both are virgins. Both Pinkie's and Rose's names are shades of the same primary colour, red. Moreover, the two frequently perceive each other as being somehow related or even interchangeable. For instance, while trying to get Rose's parents' permission to allow him to marry the girl, Pinkie feels as if he were bargaining for his own sister because with Rose's father the Boy 'heard his father speaking, that figure in the corner was his mother' (Part Five: 3): the suggestion is that Pinkie and Rose share a common psychological heritage. Pinkie even knows Rose's thoughts: 'they beat unregarded in his own nerves', as though they were his own: 'I can tell you what she's thinking of' (Part Six: 2). And when Rose returns to Snow's after her marriage, '*she* stood now where Pinkie had stood – outside, looking in. This was what the priests meant by one flesh' (Part Seven: 1). Thus, it is not surprising that while planning the suicide pact Pinkie confuses his own identity with Rose's, becoming 'uncertain who it was who had to die . . . himself or her or both . . .' (Part Seven: 5; Greene's ellipses).

On the other hand, points of opposition between Pinkie and Rose are numerous. The Boy's violent hatred, aggressive cruelty, and murderous guilt are countered by Rose's loyal love, maternal kindness, and naive innocence. She thinks about others – Pinkie, the children she is twice attracted by, the baby she might herself give birth to; Pinkie is self-centred, looking forward to the time when he will have 'nothing to think about but himself. Myself . . .' (Part Seven: 7). Rose dreams romantically about courtship, marriage and child-bearing. Pinkie's courtship of and marriage to Rose are coldly calculated, pragmatic moves designed to ensure his own safety; the possibility of Rose's pregnancy at once infuriates, disgusts and frightens him, and he asks Dallow about methods of abortion in the event that the girl really is pregnant.

Greene's purpose in presenting Pinkie and Rose as doubles is to emphasise that they represent two poles of the same religious experience. That is, they are both concerned with the same religious questions, but they approach these questions from opposite spiritual directions. Pinkie and Rose perceive life in terms of opposed religious eternals, heaven and hell, Pinkie of course being aligned with the latter and Rose with the former. For both characters, then, the physical world lay 'between two eternities. They faced each other as it were from opposite territories, but like troops at Christmas time they fraternized' (Part Five: 2). This shared concern for spiritual realms produces the 'sense of communion' Pinkie feels with Rose; the two 'Romans' 'understood each other. She used terms common to heaven and hell' (Part Six: 2). Rose attracts Pinkie because her goodness helps to define and to clarify for him his own evil, of which he is so proud: the girl 'completed him . . . What was most evil in him needed her: it couldn't get along without goodness . . . . She was good, . . . and he was damned: they were made for each other' (Part Four: 3).

Ida, in turn, represents everything that Pinkie and Rose are not. Whereas Pinkie and Rose are physically underdeveloped, childlike in appearance, and virginal, Ida is several times said to be large-breasted and broad-hipped, motherly and sensual. And whereas Pinkie and Rose represent two opposing spiritual eternities, Ida is an irreligious creature of the physical world who 'didn't believe in heaven or hell' (Part One: 3). 'That's just religion', she responds when Rose speaks of sacred matters. 'It's the world we got to deal with' (Part Seven: 1). Ida enjoys secular pleasures unashamedly – drinking, singing, gambling, love-making – trusting to her planchette, rather than to prayer, to help her through her difficulties. Indeed, Ida is an alien to the 'strange country' of the spiritual worlds of Pinkie and Rose, 'as far from either of them as she was from Hell – or Heaven' (Part Four: 3). Instead of the metaphysical 'stronger foods' of 'Good and Evil' (Part Seven: 1) of Pinkie and Rose's 'dark theology' (Part Four: 1), Ida believes only in earthly 'justice', 'fair play' and 'law and order' (Part Three: 1).

Minor characters

Spicer, Cubitt, Dallow and Prewitt: the first three of these characters are members of Pinkie's mob; the last is the gang's lawyer. Although none is developed in detail, all are given enough traits to individualise them. All of them serve in some way to forward the action and also to help characterise Pinkie.

Middle-aged, neurotic, and sentimental, Spicer plants the 'Kolley Kibber' card Rose finds at Snow's, which forces Pinkie to court and eventually to marry her. Spicer's continual worrying that the police will somehow discover the truth about Hale's death causes him to drink and smoke excessively and to break out in hives. With his painful corns and balding head, Spicer is pitiable. He constantly pleads with Pinkie to find peaceable means of achieving the mob's ends, and even Pinkie concedes that Spicer is loyal and relatively harmless. Pinkie's murder of Spicer, committed because Spicer becomes careless when scared, is unnecessary; it would have been enough simply to send Spicer out of town (as Pinkie later does with Prewitt). Spicer serves mainly to (a) complicate the plot by leaving the card at Snow's; and (b) underscore Pinkie's malicious, even sadistic, nature – before murdering Spicer, Pinkie sets a trap for him with Colleoni and feels 'rising cruelty' when he sees Spicer's bandaged cheek: the Boy wants to 'tear [the bandage] away and see the skin break' (Part Four: 1).

John Cubitt's dominant trait is his impulse to jest about sex. He is large, red-haired and freckled. Like Spicer, Cubitt drinks, and he is even fatalistic about doing so: 'What can a man do but drink?' (Part Six: 1). Cubitt supports Spicer's attempts to curb Pinkie's widening circle of violence, though he is proudly masculine about his own identity with the gang. Beneath his toughness, however, Cubitt is lonely and cheaply sentimental (he wishes he could write heart-rending love-letters), which makes him susceptible to Ida's 'large friendly bosom' (Part Six: 1). Cubitt's functions are to (a) stress Pinkie's aversion to sex (especially by way of the two obscene wedding presents he gives Pinkie); and (b) forward the action by providing Ida with crucial information.

Muscular and not intellectually bright, Ted Dallow is, after Pinkie, the most violent member of the gang. His broken nose is an indication of his pugnacity. Dallow's use of violence in the story, however, is largely restricted to his almost brutal 'angry passion' (Part Seven: 1) for his mistress, Judy (wife of Frank, the blind dry-cleaner who owns the boarding-house in which Pinkie's mob resides), and to the knife-slashing he is eager to perform; he, too, objects to more murders. Although Dallow admires the Boy to the point of following him 'like a large friendly dog' (Part Two: 1), he reacts several times against Pinkie's cruel treatment of Rose. Indeed, it is largely because Rose's efforts at keeping house awaken in him a 'sentimental desire' for domestic tranquillity the tawdry Judy cannot fulfil that Dallow helps Ida pursue Pinkie. Like Cubitt, Dallow finds comfort in Ida's oversized bosom, which is 'ready for any secrets', and Dallow 'too began automatically to confide' in Ida (Part Seven: 8). 'Dallow's creed', 'The world's all right if you don't go too far' (Part Six: 2) – though it does not satisfy Pinkie's overreaching ambition – echoes Ida's belief that 'The world was a good place if you didn't weaken' (Part Seven: 6). Again similar to Ida, Dallow denies Pinkie's religious abstractions on physical grounds, refusing to believe in hell because he cannot see it. Dallow (*a*) helps to bring the action to a climax by assisting Ida in her pursuit of Pinkie; and (*b*) highlights Pinkie's malice: even the characteristically violent Dallow thinks the Boy has gone too far with his murderous schemes.

Prewitt, Pinkie's lawyer, is a broken, middle-aged man trapped in an unhappy marriage of twenty-five years. He is forced by Pinkie to lie about Spicer's death. He, too, like Spicer and Cubitt, takes refuge in drink. And he indulges in fantasies about the 'little typists' who pass his window. Indeed, Prewitt's sexual frustration has produced a perverse exhibitionistic impulse, an 'urge to expose myself – shamefully – in a park' (Part Seven: 3). His courtroom method is deception, the 'wangle, twist, contradictory clause, ambiguous word'. Hence, Prewitt has sacrificed his personal integrity to the pursuit of professional success, so that his character – epitomised by his 'lined and wasted and unreliable face' – has 'aged in many law courts, with many victories more damaging than defeats'. Prewitt attempts to conceal his inner emptiness, betrayed by his 'hollow joviality' (Part Four: 1), behind an outpouring of high-sounding literary quotations.

Colleoni is the highly successful leader of the mob that contends with Pinkie's Bookmakers' Protection for control of the race-track extortion racket. His gang's murder of Kite (committed before the action of *Brighton Rock* begins) incites Pinkie to kill Hale, who had informed Colleoni that Kite was trying to cut in on Colleoni's criminal territory. Just as Ida embodies physical and sensual values repulsive to Pinkie, so Colleoni possesses material and financial advantages Pinkie strives mightily, though futilely, to attain. Colleoni is small, middle-aged, and well groomed and dressed, with an 'Italian face' (Part Two: 2). He considers himself to be a businessman, rather than a racketeer; but his material achievements and smooth manner cannot mask his ignorance, which is revealed by his identifying, 'vaguely', the French empress Eugenie as 'Oh, . . . one of those foreign polonies.' His 'shrewd' eyes (Part Two: 2) accent the cleverness that has guided his success – for example, the manner in which he double-crosses the unwitting Pinkie over the attack on Spicer at the race-track. Unlike the Boy, who progressively feels that he is losing control over his own affairs, Colleoni is in complete command, even, to some extent, of the police, whom he gets to take Pinkie into custody. Indeed, according to Crab, one of his gang-members, Colleoni will eventually enter politics, an ultimate instrument of institutionalised control. His functions as a device in the plot and as an aid in characterising Pinkie are discussed below, in Part 4, in the first specimen answer to question (1).

Thin, quiet, and sexually passive, perhaps even impotent, Phil Corkery is the improbable companion of the buxom, boisterous Ida in her pursuit of Pinkie. His 'stiff collar' (Part Three: 1) symbolises his strangled emotions. Ida agrees to Phil's proposal that they meet in Brighton because her planchette spells out his name and also because she needs a witness for her investigation. First counselling Ida to abandon her dangerous mission to the police and later advising her to quit because 'we've done enough' (Part Seven: 6), Phil helps to emphasise Ida's unflagging persistence.

'Fred' Hale, whose real Christian name is Charles, is an undersized newspaper-man with ink-stained fingers. His close-bitten finger nails betray his nervousness. Like other male characters in the novel, Hale is drawn to Ida because of her comforting maternal qualities. His murder by Pinkie's mob incites the forward action of the plot: this is Hale's main function in *Brighton Rock*. Hale also serves to characterise Pinkie and Ida as physical opposites: the ascetic, cold, 'starved intensity' Hale perceives in the underdeveloped Boy contrasts with the uninhibited, warm, 'friendly accommodating' manner Hale recognises in the full-bodied Ida (Part One: 1).

Generally, Greene's characterisation in *Brighton Rock* is successful. He develops his major characters in sufficient depth to make their motivations psychologically believable (Ida pursues Pinkie, for instance, not only because she feels sorry for Hale and has a keen sense of justice, but also because she feels guilty for having left Hale when she went to have a wash; wants to save Rose; and simply finds it fun to track down Hale's murderer). Greene also gives his characters enough traits to make them interesting (an example is the complex manner in which Pinkie's susceptibility to music is treated). The minor characters serve their functions in the novel unobtrusively because they are sufficiently humanised to avoid seeming to be only plot devices. And Greene is especially deft at creating effective characters who appear only very briefly – consider, for example, the presentation of Rose's parents, of Sylvie (Spicer's girl), and of the parking-lot attendant Pinkie tries to use for alibi purposes.

There are, however, some inconsistencies of characterisation in *Brighton Rock*. Pinkie, for instance, often accurately recalls from his choirboy days patches of a hymn from the Latin Mass whose meaning he understands; yet he does not seem to know the meaning of 'memento mori', or, for that matter, even to recognise it as being Latin – but he is capable of breaking out, in grammatical Latin, with 'Credo in unum Satanum' (Part Six: 2). Pinkie also occasionally has perceptions that seem improbable for a seventeen-year-old not educated beyond the board, or elementary, school level, as when he likens the complexities of his own manoeuvrings to those at the Battle of Waterloo, or as when he waxes almost poetical: 'Perhaps when they christened me, the holy water didn't take. I never howled the devil out' (Part Four: 3). Similarly, in the case of Rose, it is unlikely that a girl who has never been outside Brighton would imagine her new life at Frank's as taking place in a 'foreign land [that] absorbed her too quickly – no sooner were you past the customs than the naturalization papers were signed, you were conscripted' (Part Seven: 1); or, even more improbably, that she would consider her possible suicide to be a 'romantic adventure' like the Spanish Civil War: 'you plan to fight in Spain, and then before you know the tickets are taken for you, the introductions are pressed into your hand, somebody has come to see you off, everything is real' (Part Seven: 9).

The language

Each of the major characters has a language appropriate to his established character. Pinkie's language is cold, clipped, functional – just like his actions. He uses simple words of one or two syllables and uncomplicated syntax (usually subject–predicate–object). With a few notable exceptions, such as his description of hell ('Flames and damnation . . . torments' [Part Two: 1]), Pinkie's language is generally sparse in imagery, revealing his lack of aesthetic sensibility (the Boy's 'imagination hadn't awoken' [Part Two: 1]). What does give some flavour to Pinkie's language are its race-track slang and vulgarisms. For example, Pinkie seldom uses the word 'girl', instead referring to females as 'tarts', 'buers', and 'polonies'. His frequent witticisms are characteristically muted and often cruel, rather than humorous, as when he recites the she-loves-me, she-loves-me-not formula while plucking the legs and wings off an insect, and then tells Spicer that he has just had a date with Rose. Pinkie does, however, occasionally recall parts of the Latin Mass, which provides a striking opposition to his usual linguistic habits: while his normally unrefined use of language reveals a coarse, even vulgar sensibility, his recollection of Latin suggests the more dignified, useful life he might have led had he kept his boyhood vow to become a priest.

The predominant feature of Rose's language is its occasional romanticism, which helps stress the polar oppositions (such as heaven and hell) between Rose and Pinkie. Usually, she uses simple, colloquial language consistent with her background, situation and character. But when aroused by her love for Pinkie, she becomes sentimental, using a language appropriate to her inflated emotions. On their first date, for example, Rose describes Sherry's as 'lovely', even though it is only a common dance hall (Part Two: 1). And when Pinkie takes her to Peacehaven, she repeats the adjective: 'It's lovely, . . . being out here – in the country, with you' – again, even though the landscape is pictured as being unattractive, and even though Pinkie is a shabby thug (Part Three: 3). Similarly, to Pinkie's question of whether she would like to be his girl, Rose replies that she would 'love it' (Part Two: 1). Even the Boy's cruelty can elicit a romantic response from Rose: she thinks Pinkie 'sweet', even though she realises he has just insulted her (Part Three: 3). Rose's tendency to speak in absolutes also reveals the romantic exaggeration that controls her perceptions, as when she tells Pinkie that she will 'never, never, never' let him down (Part Four: 3).

Ida's language suggests the combination of good-natured joy of living and stern righteousness that constitutes her character. Her loud and boisterous manner in pubs, the pleasure she takes in singing sentimental ballads, and the drink-induced belches and laughter that frequently accompany her words show her light side. On the other hand, her more serious side is manifested in the moralistic aphorisms that Ida clicks out automatically, 'like a ticket from a slot machine' (Part Seven: 1), for example, 'Waste not, want not' (Part Three: 1). She carries a ready stock of such slogans about fair play, not letting the innocent suffer, eye-for-an-eye vengeance, and law and order, for use at appropriate moments. Ida's unbending sense of justice is further evident in the lectures she delivers to Rose. On these occasions Ida's language can be fervently exhortative as she commands the girl to renounce Pinkie. Finally, Ida can modulate her language from maternal gentleness to threatening forcefulness to achieve her ends, as with Cubitt and Dallow.

The minor characters – even those who appear only for a single episode – also use language shaped to their personalities, and Greene provides linguistic traits that help to individualise them. For example, Sylvie's shallowness is exposed by her repeated overstatements, which veil her promiscuity behind childishly naive exaggeration. 'Oh gosh, how wonderful' it will be when Pinkie finally takes a fancy to girls; 'O gosh, wouldn't it be fine?' to go out to the cars with Pinkie. She also has appropriately childish nicknames for her male friends; so Spicer, to her, is 'Spicie', and Dallow, 'Dallie' (Part Five: 1). The priest, to whom Rose confesses, also shows Greene's skilful use of language to sketch credible minor characters. Using the sermon technique of the exemplum, the priest gives a specific case – the example of the Frenchman – to illustrate a general truth – the inconceivable mystery of God's grace. He draws on the Bible and a Latin proverb to explain his points. And the possibility that his comforting words are actually empty is implied in the way the priest speaks to Rose 'mechanically' (Part Seven: 11).

Part 4

Hints for study

General

Above all else, you should read *Brighton Rock* as many times and as carefully as possible. To read the novel carefully, you must read actively, as opposed to passively. That is, instead of simply beginning with the first word and reading straight through until you arrive at the last word, learn to think as you read about such matters as structure, theme, language and characterisation, to isolate key episodes, to note down recurring images and motifs. To do these things, you can, for example, underline crucial passages, make interpretative comments in the book's margins, and list separately, by page number, material that is repeated. After you have done these things, go back over the novel, trying to pull together whatever particulars seem to you to be significant in order to see what patterns emerge. As narrative literature is almost always shaped in terms of conflict, you should determine who the protagonist (the main character) is; who or what the antagonist (the person with whom or force with which the protagonist must contend) is; and what the crucial conflict between these two is. Try to arrive at an overall view of the whole book – that is, decide what the novel is about, what its total effect is. Then go back over the novel once again to see how the particulars – the episodes, the characters, the images, and so forth – that make up the whole of the work help to elucidate the work's total effect. Finally, using a good dictionary and whatever other reference tools are necessary (here a dictionary of literary terms is indispensable – a good one is M. H. Abrams (ed.), *A Glossary of Literary Terms*, fourth edition, Holt, Rinehart and Winston, New York and London, 1981), you should look up all unfamiliar words and allusions not covered in the 'Notes and Glossary' sections.

If asked to write a research paper on *Brighton Rock*, you will, of course, have to consult secondary sources to see what critics have said about the novel. You will probably be wise, however, to avoid consulting critics until after you have arrived at, and written down, your own interpretation; this will allow you to think independently about the book, without being influenced by someone else's ideas. You should keep in mind that what your instructor is striving for is to help his students learn to analyse, to argue about, and to evaluate literary texts on their own. When you do turn to secondary sources, do not accept blindly anything and everything you read: question the arguments of critics to see whether or not they are convincingly and accurately supported by textual evidence. And if in your paper you use material from a critical work, even if it is not in the form of direct quotation, you must cite the source.

If asked to answer a test question about *Brighton Rock*, analyse the question carefully before you begin to write to make certain that you understand what you are being asked to do. Then make sure that you answer the question precisely as it is asked. If the question reads, for example, 'Compare and contrast the structure of *Brighton Rock* with that of any other novel by Greene', do not start talking about Greene's life, or about his religious views, or about anything else except the structure of the two novels. Nor should you devote four-fifths of your answer to one of the novels and only one-fifth to the other – the question implies some balance in the amount of attention to be given to each work. And make sure that you actually do compare and contrast the structure of the two novels – do not merely analyse the structure of *Brighton Rock*, then that of the other novel (or, even worse, substitute a summary of the plot for a structural analysis), without pointing out significant areas of similarity and/or difference. In brief, take care that everything the question asks is covered in your answer, and that everything in your answer in some way contributes toward answering the question. If you have answered the question clearly and consistently, a reader of your answer should be able to guess, at least in general terms, what the question is. If he cannot do this, you have probably not stated your purpose clearly in your answer nor stuck consistently to the task the question has set for you. You might try checking your ability to write with unity (oneness of purpose) and coherency (relatedness of the parts to the whole) by asking someone else to read a sample answer you have prepared and to determine from it, as precisely as possible, the question it is answering.

Whether you are writing a research paper or an answer to an examination question, you should strive to be as concrete as possible – that is, to define abstractions and to support generalisations with specific details from or references to the text. If, for example, you are asked to determine whether or not *Brighton Rock* is a romantic novel, you must first define, for the purposes of your essay, what 'romantic' means. And if in discussing *Brighton Rock* as a romantic novel you point out Pinkie's alienation as one of the book's romantic characteristics, be sure to provide supporting examples for your statement – for instance, that the Boy's parents are both dead, that Pinkie has no guardian, and that he is not even registered with the municipal authorities; that to Rose the building Pinkie lives in resembles a 'house for sale' (Part Seven: 1); and that Pinkie's real Christian name is never given. As these instances show, you need not quote the text in order to support your observations; even if you are not allowed to use your book to answer a question, you should be familiar enough with the text to recall sufficient key material to be able to answer whatever question you are asked.

Finally, remember that re-reading is part of the writing process. If you are writing an examination paper, be sure to leave some time toward the end of the examination to go back over your answer. One good way to help to prepare yourself for writing under the pressure of an examination and still leaving some time for re-reading is to make up a question, then to set an alarm clock for the period of time the test will cover and to answer that question – and re-read what you have written – by the time the alarm rings.

Study topics

If you give sufficient thought to the following topics, you should be able to answer almost any question you are liable to be asked about *Brighton Rock*, including those below.

Think about the tone of *Brighton Rock*. Is it static, or does it change from episode to episode, depending upon which characters are involved? How would you characterise the overall tone of the novel: is it positive or negative?

The structure of the novel deserves attention. The story begins and ends at points of violent climax involving death, and there is another death precisely in the middle of the story. Notice also that Greene uses the detective story's structural device of delayed exposition – the motive for Hale's murder, for example, is not revealed until a quarter of the way through the novel (Part Two: 2). Consider the seven-part division of the action – why has the author made such a division? Can you represent the structure of *Brighton Rock* by means of a diagram?

Could the novel's point of view have been more effectively handled? For instance, would *Brighton Rock* be more psychologically intense were its narration limited solely to Pinkie's consciousness? What might have been the consequence had Greene limited the story to Ida's perspective? Had Greene used either solely Pinkie's or solely Ida's point of view, would the story be more effective than in its actual form?

The language of the novel should also be considered. How would you classify Greene's style in *Brighton Rock* – colloquial or formal, simple or complex? Notice that a large portion of the narrative is conducted by means of dialogue – what effect does this produce? What are the novel's key recurring images, and what do they contribute to the story?

Are the particular characters static ('flat') or dynamic ('round'), that is, do they change significantly, or are they essentially the same at the end of the novel as they were at the beginning? Does anyone learn anything in *Brighton Rock*, and if so, who learns what, and how does he learn it? And if not, why not? Examine some of the minor characters not commented on above, for instance, Kite and Judy. What are their functions in the novel?

Why do you think Greene has selected Brighton as the setting for the novel? Consider those passages in which the city is described – what atmosphere does the Brighton setting provide, and how appropriate is it to the whole of the story?

Some possible questions

1. Point out the contributions the character of Colleoni makes to *Brighton Rock*.
2. One of the main features of *Brighton Rock* is its irony. Investigate the functions of irony in the novel.
3. Discuss the function of the old man who stoops down several times on the beach.
4. Discuss Pinkie as an anti-hero.
5. Several critics have argued that the reader is really not supposed to sympathise with Ida's eye-for-an-eye, I'm-on-the-side-of-Right brand of justice. Are these critics correct or not?
6. Are the words of the priest who appears at the end of the novel meant to be taken at face value, or are they meant ironically? Explain how you have arrived at your conclusion.
7. Apart from Part One: 1, *Brighton Rock* is told from the point of view of either Pinkie, Rose, Ida, or an omniscient narrator, with two exceptions: Part Three: 2 is told from Spicer's viewpoint and Part Six: 1 from Cubitt's. Why has Greene shifted the point of view in these cases, and are the shifts justifiable?
8. Analyse the scraps of song, and Pinkie's reaction to them, that Ida sings throughout the novel. Determine what, if anything, the songs have in common; how they serve to characterise Ida; and what they reveal about the Boy.
9. When Greene transformed the novel into a screenplay, he altered the ending. In the film the message Pinkie records is worded differently from that in the novel: 'You want me to say I love you. Here's the truth. I hate you, you little slut.' The film ends with Rose actually playing the record, but with the phonograph becoming stuck just as Pinkie says, 'I love you', so that these three words are repeated over and over, with the camera focusing on a picture of the crucifixion as the film ends. Compare and contrast this revised ending with the ending Greene wrote for the novel, arguing which is the more effective.

10. Images of the following recur frequently in *Brighton Rock*: religion; music; battle; sickness (including poison); school; animal; entrapment. Discuss one of these kinds of imagery in detail, showing what it contributes to the whole of the novel.

11. Show how the literary (including the biblical) allusions contribute to the total effect of *Brighton Rock*.

12. Analyse the time-scheme of the novel. Why has Greene used such a time-scheme? Discuss the significance of Whitsun in your answer.

13. Discuss the satirical elements of *Brighton Rock*.

14. Point out the importance of one of the following episodes: (*a*) Hale's funeral; (*b*) Pinkie's meeting with Colleoni; (*c*) the trip to the Queen of Hearts made by Dallow, Cubitt, and Pinkie; (*d*) the stop for drinks Pinkie and Rose make at the Peacehaven hotel.

15. Select a key statement made by one of the novels' characters and show how it can be considered a microcosm of *Brighton Rock*.

Planning your answer

Suppose you have been asked to write on the first of the above questions: 'Point out the contributions the character of Colleoni makes to *Brighton Rock*.' The first step in preparing your answer is to look closely at the question itself to see what you are really being asked to do. The question asks you to do one task only – to discuss the functions of Colleoni in the novel.

The next step is to plan your answer. Some students do this best by simply jotting down a few ideas; others rely on more formal methods, such as outlining. In any event, like most questions, this one suggests an organisational pattern for an answer. You can begin with a general statement on the two or three most significant functions of Colleoni, then proceed by developing your essay with specific details that will support this central idea.

Specimen answers

1. Point out the contributions the character of Colleoni makes to *Brighton Rock*.

ANSWER (A):

Colleoni's chief contributions as a character in Graham Greene's *Brighton Rock* are two: Colleoni functions as a device in the plot; and he helps to characterise one of the major figures in the novel, Pinkie.

As a device in the plot, Colleoni provides background information, melodrama and social criticism. To begin with, the introduction of Colleoni into the story reveals the motivation for the murder of Hale:

Hale had told Colleoni that Kite, the former leader of Pinkie's mob, was cutting in on Colleoni's racket. Further, Colleoni contributes to the novel's melodrama in the scene in which Pinkie sets up Spicer to be murdered by Colleoni's gang, only to find himself the victim of a violent demonstration of Colleoni's power. Thirdly, as a favourite of the Conservative party who will eventually himself enter politics, Colleoni provides an implied criticism of a society in which businesslike criminals (Colleoni considers himself a businessman, rather than an outlaw) ironically gain control of the law-making body politic. Even the social institution entrusted with enforcing the law – the police – trust Colleoni.

But more than being only a device in the plot, Colleoni develops Pinkie's character by helping to reveal the Boy's pride and ambition. Pinkie's pride is in the power he convinces himself that he has, but to which Colleoni's vastly superior power gives the lie. Pinkie's pride is badly hurt during his meeting with Colleoni, in which Colleoni three times refers to Pinkie as a child, patronising him with fatherly advice and even offering him a job. Worse, as Pinkie leaves Colleoni's, the police apprehend him – at, the Boy realises, Colleoni's request – to try to talk him into leaving Brighton because he cannot stand up against Colleoni. Leaving the police station, Pinkie proudly vows to assert himself on a world scale, even though the local police acknowledge Colleoni as the power behind Brighton crime.

Pinkie's ambition is for the material opulence Colleoni displays, which contrasts blatantly with his own filthy surroundings. When Pinkie first learns that Colleoni is staying in a suite of the high-class Cosmopolitan Hotel, he is given a bitter reminder of his own cheap, crumb-strewn room at Frank's. The interview with Colleoni also emphasises Pinkie's materialism. The Boy is attracted by the expensive, plush details of Colleoni's office, even by Colleoni's gold cigar lighter. But again the display of wealth only underscores for Pinkie his great distance from the material goals to which he aspires. Indeed, it is an indication of Pinkie's obsessions with power and wealth that he is occasionally haunted by visions of Colleoni's luxury in contrast with his own pitiful circumstances.

COMMENT: This response consistently answers the question. It announces clearly its central idea and organisational pattern at the start, then develops that central idea logically and convincingly, moving from less significant points to more important ones. Notice that, although the answer continually gives textual examples, it contains no quotations. The answer can be broken down into an outline that reveals how its writer gathered together particular details to support his argument:

Central idea: Colleoni has two functions.
1.   Colleoni is a device in the plot.

(a) He provides background information about Kite.

(b) He contributes melodrama in the race-track episode.

(c) He is a source of social criticism of politics and the police.

2. Colleoni helps to develop Pinkie's character.

(a) He shows that Pinkie's pride of power is unjustified (Pinkie is insulted during his interview with Colleoni; Colleoni is able to use the police against Pinkie).

(b) He reveals the gap between Pinkie's lust for material possessions and Pinkie's own dismal surroundings (Pinkie is jealous of Colleoni's wealth even before he meets Colleoni; at Colleoni's, Pinkie realises that the wealth he sees is beyond his reach; the Boy is haunted by the luxury surrounding Colleoni, which he himself lacks).

ANSWER (B):

Although not a main character in *Brighton Rock*, Colleoni does play a role in the novel. He has come to Brighton for a weekend, presumably to look after the activities of his gang. He requests a meeting with the leader of the rival Bookmakers' Protection gang, expressing surprise when he is confronted with the seventeen-year-old Pinkie Brown, rather than with Kite. However, Colleoni is only pretending ignorance – he knows that Kite is, in fact, dead, for it was his own mob that murdered him. Colleoni impresses Pinkie greatly with his ostentatious display of silver and gold, making it clear that such a world of luxury does not include people like Pinkie. Colleoni has called the meeting with Pinkie in answer to Pinkie's razor-slashing of Brewer, a bookie whom Pinkie has punished for transferring his race-track protection payments from Pinkie's mob to Colleoni's. Colleoni overtly wants to warn Pinkie against interfering in his 'business'; but covertly he is telling Pinkie to give up the protection racket altogether because he, Colleoni, is after a monopoly against which Pinkie is powerless. Colleoni gets the police to pick up Pinkie as the Boy is leaving the Cosmopolitan in a further effort to convince him to give up his racket. Although Colleoni does not reappear physically in the novel, he is mentioned later. After Pinkie telephones Colleoni to set up Spicer, he feels again the pull of Colleoni's wealth, as against his own low-grade way of life. Then at the track Colleoni double-crosses the Boy by ordering his men to attack Pinkie, as well as Spicer, with razors. Pinkie flees, crying with pain and deeply insulted. Finally, Crab tells Cubitt that Colleoni might in future enter politics and that the Conservative party is impressed by his contacts.

COMMENT: This answer is unsatisfactory because it lacks focus. It asserts at the beginning that Colleoni 'plays a role' in *Brighton Rock*, but never states what that role is. Hence, all that follows really does not develop any idea – indeed, it merely summarises, in a single lengthy paragraph, most of the action in which Colleoni is directly or indirectly involved. Notice, however, that the summary is specific, so that much of the material it contains could be used to write a satisfactory answer, if only that material were related to a clearly stated focal point.

---

2. One of the main features of *Brighton Rock* is its irony. Investigate the functions of irony in the novel.

If irony denotes a discrepancy between what is meant, either in speech or in deed, and what actually happens, then Greene's *Brighton Rock* is heavily ironic. The chief function of irony in the novel is to emphasise the futility of all Pinkie's actions, in contrast to the significant impact Pinkie believes he will make on the world. This irony can be seen in Pinkie's image of himself, in his relationship with Rose, and in his fate at Ida's hands.

There is always a gap between Pinkie's vision of himself and his real position, and that gap increases as the novel progresses. Always proudly ambitious, Pinkie begins by imagining a 'great future' for himself, even though he is only the leader of a small-time mob that is falling apart and being run out of business. Pinkie's lofty estimate of himself is put into ironic perspective at one point when he enters his room: 'his pallid face peered dimly back at him full of pride from the mirror over the ewer, the soap dish, the basin of stale water'. Later, Pinkie himself views his possible sexual intercourse with Sylvie ironically, seeing 'his enormous ambitions under the shadow of the hideous and commonplace act'. Ironically impotent, Pinkie – the 'top', a 'conqueror' whose 'breast ached with the effort to enclose the whole world' – retches.

Pinkie's relationship with Rose helps to undercut his unwarranted self-esteem. At first thinking himself too important to marry and start a family, Pinkie instead is 'going to be where Colleoni now was and higher'. Yet Pinkie of course very shortly marries Rose and perhaps even makes her pregnant. Further, Pinkie's claim, made just before he kisses Rose for the first time, of complete knowledge about the details of sex is undercut by the fact that he has not yet even kissed a girl. As it becomes clear that Pinkie will have to marry Rose for the sake of his own safety, he himself sees the incongruity between the greatness he associates with his own character on the one hand, and marriage to Rose on the other: 'but this – the cheapest, the youngest, the most inexperienced skirt in all Brighton – to have *me* in her power'. And, ironically, the more Pinkie tries to control Rose, the more he himself becomes controlled by circumstances; although he believes he has extricated himself permanently from the slums of his boyhood, for example, he must return to them to ask Rose's parents for her hand, so that his relationship with Rose is a form of social 'retreat'. A further irony connected with Pinkie's unwanted marriage is that, as Dallow tells the Boy, 'It was your own doing': had he not gone to Snow's against the wishes of his mob to try to retrieve the Kolley Kibber card Spicer had left there, Pinkie would not have become involved with Rose. And more: Pinkie's marriage to Rose, far from increasing his safety, only provides Ida with another motive – saving the girl – to hunt Pinkie down. Finally, Pinkie's death – an indirect result of his refusal to believe that Rose will not turn against him – is unnecessary because, as Dallow points out, Rose is totally trustworthy. Pinkie marries Rose to gain safety; then plots her death, also to gain safety – yet when the novel ends, Rose is alive and Pinkie dead. Hence, the novel's grimmest irony is Pinkie's thought, 'If he married her at all, of course, it wouldn't be long', as of course it is not, but in a way very different from Pinkie's anticipation.

It is Pinkie's ironic misperception of Ida that most emphatically negates the Boy's inflated picture of himself. For Pinkie, Ida 'don't matter' because 'She's just nothing.' Yet it is of course Ida who tracks Pinkie down – which she is able to do, ironically, with the money she wins at the race-track, supposedly Pinkie's stronghold. And the horse Ida successfully bets on, Black Boy, is a long shot to which Hale had tipped her off, so that the very man Pinkie destroys becomes himself a tool for the destruction of Pinkie.

The novel's culminating irony is Pinkie's unintended suicide. Not only does it occur instead of the suicide Pinkie had planned so carefully to trick Rose into, not only do the three characters who pursue Pinkie know where he is because of the alibis he himself had established, and not only is the suicide brought about by his own vitriol; Pinkie's suicide also ironically recalls his misperception of Ida. For it is Pinkie, who had viewed Ida as a cipher and himself as all-mighty, whose life in the end adds up to nil. When Pinkie leaps over the cliff to his death, the other characters present 'couldn't hear a splash. It was as if he'd been withdrawn suddenly by a hand out of any existence – past or present, whipped away into zero – nothing'.

COMMENT: This essay satisfies the assignment. It answers the question as it is asked; defines the key abstraction, irony; states clearly at the start what main point will be made and how it will be developed; and develops that point with specific references from the text. It does not digress or toss in irrelevancies: everything it contains serves in some way to answer the question.

Now choose one of the questions above not answered here, respond to it, and then write a commentary analysing your answer.

Part 5

Suggestions for further reading

The text

These Notes use the readily available Penguin edition of *Brighton Rock*:

GREENE, GRAHAM: *Brighton Rock*, Penguin Books, Harmondsworth, 1975.

Important hardbound editions are:

GREENE, GRAHAM: *Brighton Rock*, Viking, New York, 1938; reissued 1948.
GREENE, GRAHAM: *Brighton Rock*, Heinemann, London, 1938.
GREENE, GRAHAM: *Brighton Rock*, Heinemann, London, 1950 (Uniform Edition).
GREENE, GRAHAM: *Brighton Rock*, Bodley Head, London, 1970 (Collected Edition). (This includes an Introduction by Greene.)

Other works by Greene

Greene's own non-fiction works are often helpful in understanding his novels. The convenient Penguin editions of the following contain material pertinent to *Brighton Rock*:

GREENE, GRAHAM: *The Lawless Roads*, Penguin Books, Harmondsworth, 1947. (In the Prologue, Greene discusses the miseries of his schoolboy days.)
GREENE, GRAHAM: *Collected Essays*, Penguin Books, Harmondsworth, 1970. (This includes the essay 'The Lost Childhood', which is especially recommended.)
GREENE, GRAHAM: *A Sort of Life*, Penguin Books, Harmondsworth, 1972. (This volume of autobiography covers Greene's early years.)
GREENE, GRAHAM: *Ways of Escape*, Penguin Books, Harmondsworth, 1981. (This volume of autobiography covers the later years, and reprints Greene's Introduction to *Brighton Rock*.)

Works about Greene

BEEBE, MAURICE: 'Criticism of Graham Greene: A selected Checklist with an Index to Studies of Separate Works', *Modern Fiction Studies*, 3 (Autumn 1957), pp. 281-8.

BRENNAN, NEIL: 'Bibliography', in *Graham Greene: Some Critical Observations*, ed. Robert O. Evans, University of Kentucky Press, Lexington, 1967, pp. 245–76. (This collection also contains essays pertinent to *Brighton Rock*.)

COSTA, RICHARD HAUER: 'Graham Greene', in *British Novelists, 1930–1959*, ed. Bernard Oldsey, vol. 13 of *The Dictionary of Literary Biography*, Gale Research, Detroit, Michigan, 1982. (The most recent brief survey of Greene's work.)

HYNES, SAMUEL (ED.): *Graham Greene: A Collection of Critical Essays*, Prentice-Hall, Englewood Cliffs, New Jersey, 1973. (This also contains material pertinent to *Brighton Rock*.)

PHILIPS, GENE D., S.J.: *Graham Greene: The Films of His Fiction*, Teachers College Press, New York and London 1974. (This study compares the novel's ending with the ending Greene wrote for the film.)

VANN, DON J.: *Graham Greene: A Checklist of Criticism*, Kent State University Press, Kent, Ohio, 1970. (This bibliography includes references to reviews of *Brighton Rock*.)

The author of these notes

MICHAEL ROUTH was educated at California State University, Long Beach, the University of Southern California, and the University of Wisconsin. He has taught at Texas A&M University, the University of Tampere (Finland), and the University of Utrecht. He has published articles in various scholarly journals and is at present writing a critical study of the American novelist William March. He is also the author of York Notes on Aldous Huxley's *Brave New World*.

York Notes: list of titles

CHINUA ACHEBE
Things Fall Apart
EDWARD ALBEE
Who's Afraid of Virginia Woolf?
ANONYMOUS
Beowulf
Everyman
W. H. AUDEN
Selected Poems
JANE AUSTEN
Emma
Mansfield Park
Northanger Abbey
Persuasion
Pride and Prejudice
Sense and Sensibility
SAMUEL BECKETT
Waiting for Godot
ARNOLD BENNETT
The Card
JOHN BETJEMAN
Selected Poems
WILLIAM BLAKE
Songs of Innocence, Songs of Experience
ROBERT BOLT
A Man For All Seasons
HAROLD BRIGHOUSE
Hobson's Choice
ANNE BRONTË
The Tenant of Wildfell Hall
CHARLOTTE BRONTË
Jane Eyre
EMILY BRONTË
Wuthering Heights
ROBERT BROWNING
Men and Women
JOHN BUCHAN
The Thirty-Nine Steps
JOHN BUNYAN
The Pilgrim's Progress
BYRON
Selected Poems
GEOFFREY CHAUCER
Prologue to the Canterbury Tales
The Clerk's Tale
The Franklin's Tale
The Knight's Tale
The Merchant's Tale
The Miller's Tale
The Nun's Priest's Tale

The Pardoner's Tale
The Wife of Bath's Tale
Troilus and Criseyde
SAMUEL TAYLOR COLERIDGE
Selected Poems
SIR ARTHUR CONAN DOYLE
The Hound of the Baskervilles
WILLIAM CONGREVE
The Way of the World
JOSEPH CONRAD
Heart of Darkness
STEPHEN CRANE
The Red Badge of Courage
BRUCE DAWE
Selected Poems
DANIEL DEFOE
Moll Flanders
Robinson Crusoe
WALTER DE LA MARE
Selected Poems
SHELAGH DELANEY
A Taste of Honey
CHARLES DICKENS
A Tale of Two Cities
Bleak House
David Copperfield
Great Expectations
Hard Times
Oliver Twist
The Pickwick Papers
EMILY DICKINSON
Selected Poems
JOHN DONNE
Selected Poems
GERALD DURRELL
My Family and Other Animals
GEORGE ELIOT
Middlemarch
Silas Marner
The Mill on the Floss
T. S. ELIOT
Four Quartets
Murder in the Cathedral
Selected Poems
The Cocktail Party
The Waste Land
J. G. FARRELL
The Siege of Krishnapur
WILLIAM FAULKNER
The Sound and the Fury

HENRY FIELDING
Joseph Andrews
Tom Jones

F. SCOTT FITZGERALD
Tender is the Night
The Great Gatsby

GUSTAVE FLAUBERT
Madame Bovary

E. M. FORSTER
A Passage to India
Howards End

JOHN FOWLES
The French Lieutenant's Woman

JOHN GALSWORTHY
Strife

MRS GASKELL
North and South

WILLIAM GOLDING
Lord of the Flies
The Spire

OLIVER GOLDSMITH
She Stoops to Conquer
The Vicar of Wakefield

ROBERT GRAVES
Goodbye to All That

GRAHAM GREENE
Brighton Rock
The Heart of the Matter
The Power and the Glory

WILLIS HALL
The Long and the Short and the Tall

THOMAS HARDY
Far from the Madding Crowd
Jude the Obscure
Selected Poems
Tess of the D'Urbervilles
The Mayor of Casterbridge
The Return of the Native
The Woodlanders

L. P. HARTLEY
The Go-Between

NATHANIEL HAWTHORNE
The Scarlet Letter

SEAMUS HEANEY
Selected Poems

ERNEST HEMINGWAY
A Farewell to Arms
The Old Man and the Sea

SUSAN HILL
I'm the King of the Castle

BARRY HINES
Kes

HOMER
The Iliad
The Odyssey

GERARD MANLEY HOPKINS
Selected Poems

TED HUGHES
Selected Poems

ALDOUS HUXLEY
Brave New World

HENRIK IBSEN
A Doll's House

HENRY JAMES
The Portrait of a Lady
Washington Square

BEN JONSON
The Alchemist
Volpone

JAMES JOYCE
A Portrait of the Artist as a Young Man
Dubliners

JOHN KEATS
Selected Poems

PHILIP LARKIN
Selected Poems

D. H. LAWRENCE
Selected Short Stories
Sons and Lovers
The Rainbow
Women in Love

HARPER LEE
To Kill a Mocking-Bird

LAURIE LEE
Cider with Rosie

CHRISTOPHER MARLOWE
Doctor Faustus

HERMAN MELVILLE
Moby Dick

THOMAS MIDDLETON and
   WILLIAM ROWLEY
The Changeling

ARTHUR MILLER
A View from the Bridge
Death of a Salesman
The Crucible

JOHN MILTON
Paradise Lost I & II
Paradise Lost IV & IX
Selected Poems

V. S. NAIPAUL
A House for Mr Biswas

ROBERT O'BRIEN
Z for Zachariah

SEAN O'CASEY
Juno and the Paycock

GEORGE ORWELL
Animal Farm
Nineteen Eighty-four

JOHN OSBORNE
Look Back in Anger
WILFRED OWEN
Selected Poems
ALAN PATON
Cry, The Beloved Country
THOMAS LOVE PEACOCK
Nightmare Abbey and *Crotchet Castle*
HAROLD PINTER
The Caretaker
SYLVIA PLATH
Selected Works
PLATO
The Republic
ALEXANDER POPE
Selected Poems
J. B. PRIESTLEY
An Inspector Calls
WILLIAM SHAKESPEARE
A Midsummer Night's Dream
Antony and Cleopatra
As You Like It
Coriolanus
Hamlet
Henry IV Part I
Henry IV Part II
Henry V
Julius Caesar
King Lear
Macbeth
Measure for Measure
Much Ado About Nothing
Othello
Richard II
Richard III
Romeo and Juliet
Sonnets
The Merchant of Venice
The Taming of the Shrew
The Tempest
The Winter's Tale
Troilus and Cressida
Twelfth Night
GEORGE BERNARD SHAW
Arms and the Man
Candida
Pygmalion
Saint Joan
The Devil's Disciple
MARY SHELLEY
Frankenstein
PERCY BYSSHE SHELLEY
Selected Poems
RICHARD BRINSLEY SHERIDAN
The Rivals

R. C. SHERRIFF
Journey's End
JOHN STEINBECK
Of Mice and Men
The Grapes of Wrath
The Pearl
LAURENCE STERNE
A Sentimental Journey
Tristram Shandy
TOM STOPPARD
Professional Foul
Rosencrantz and Guildenstern are Dead
JONATHAN SWIFT
Gulliver's Travels
JOHN MILLINGTON SYNGE
The Playboy of the Western World
TENNYSON
Selected Poems
W. M. THACKERAY
Vanity Fair
J. R. R. TOLKIEN
The Hobbit
MARK TWAIN
Huckleberry Finn
Tom Sawyer
VIRGIL
The Aeneid
ALICE WALKER
The Color Purple
KEITH WATERHOUSE
Billy Liar
EVELYN WAUGH
Decline and Fall
JOHN WEBSTER
The Duchess of Malfi
OSCAR WILDE
The Importance of Being Earnest
THORNTON WILDER
Our Town
TENNESSEE WILLIAMS
The Glass Menagerie
VIRGINIA WOOLF
Mrs Dalloway
To the Lighthouse
WILLIAM WORDSWORTH
Selected Poems
WILLIAM WYCHERLEY
The Country Wife
W. B. YEATS
Selected Poems

York Handbooks: list of titles

YORK HANDBOOKS form a companion series to York Notes and are designed to meet the wider needs of students of English and related fields. Each volume is a compact study of a given subject area, written by an authority with experience in communicating the essential ideas to students at all levels.

AN INTRODUCTORY GUIDE TO ENGLISH LITERATURE
by MARTIN STEPHEN
PREPARING FOR EXAMINATIONS IN ENGLISH LITERATURE
by NEIL MCEWAN
READING THE SCREEN
An Introduction to Film Studies
by JOHN IZOD
ENGLISH POETRY
by CLIVE T. PROBYN
ENGLISH USAGE
by COLIN G. HEY
ENGLISH GRAMMAR
by LORETO TODD
AN INTRODUCTION TO LINGUISTICS
by LORETO TODD
AN INTRODUCTION TO LITERARY CRITICISM
by RICHARD DUTTON
A DICTIONARY OF LITERARY TERMS
by MARTIN GRAY
STUDYING CHAUCER
by ELISABETH BREWER
STUDYING SHAKESPEARE
by MARTIN STEPHEN *and* PHILIP FRANKS
STUDYING JANE AUSTEN
by IAN MILLIGAN
STUDYING THE BRONTËS
by SHEILA SULLIVAN
STUDYING CHARLES DICKENS
by K. J. FIELDING
STUDYING THOMAS HARDY
by LANCE ST JOHN BUTLER
A CHRONOLOGY OF ENGLISH LITERATURE
by MARTIN GRAY
A DICTIONARY OF BRITISH AND IRISH AUTHORS
by ANTONY KAMM
AN A.B.C. OF SHAKESPEARE
by P. C. BAYLEY
THE METAPHYSICAL POETS
by TREVOR JAMES
THE AGE OF ROMANTIC LITERATURE
by HARRY BLAMIRES